# Something w

Cassidy's thoughts flew to the young boy and the man trying to be his father. She'd sensed an unusual stiffness between the two. Not that it was any of her business. But still, her oddly electric connection with Tyson St. John, combined with the unusual way his stepson had touched something she'd kept buried deep inside, bothered Cassidy.

*You're here to do a job—not get sidetracked by a good-looking man and his son.*

But as her brain conjured up an image of Ty leaning against the counter, winking at her, she felt her pulse flutter in response.

*Don't even go there*, she ordered herself. *Just focus on your future.*

**Books by Lois Richer**

## *LOIS RICHER*

likes variety. From her time in human resources management to entrepreneurship, life has held plenty of surprises.

"Having given up on fairy tales, I was happily involved in building a restaurant when a handsome prince walked into my life and upset all my career plans with a wedding ring. Motherhood quickly followed. I guess the seeds of my storytelling took root because of two small boys who kept demanding "Then what, Mom?"

The miracle of God's love for His children, the blessing of true love, the joy of sharing Him with others—that is a story that can be told a thousand ways and yet still be brand new. Lois Richer intends to go right on telling it.

# Heart's Haven
## Lois Richer

Steeple
Hill®

Published by Steeple Hill Books™

STEEPLE HILL BOOKS

Steeple
Hill®

ISBN-13: 978-0-373-87471-2
ISBN-10:     0-373-87471-5

HEART'S HAVEN

www.SteepleHill.com

**Printed in U.S.A.**

The Lord your God is with you,
He is mighty to save.
He will take great delight in you,
He will quiet you with his love,
He will rejoice over you with singing.
—*Zephaniah* 3:17

# Chapter One

*Chicago*
*January 2*

Six years with temperamental chefs in kitchens around the world had not prepared Cassidy Preston for this.

Like fingernails on a chalkboard, the scraping of steel against steel scratched through a blue-gray fog. Smoke swirled within her throat, filling her nostrils with the acrid stench of— porridge? Cassidy wrinkled her nose to block it from her lungs.

Wincing at the painful din, Cassidy stepped across the littered room and grabbed the battered pot from the man's hand. She then scanned the kitchen, found and flicked a wall switch. The exhaust fan wheezed to life and the smoke cleared, allowing her to peer into eyes so richly blue she might have been back in Greece, staring into the Aegean.

"Excuse me."

"Certainly." Long, elegant fingers dropped the slotted spoon he'd been using as a pot scraper. He pressed a hip against the center island, tilted his head to one side. "You're excused. Now may I have that back?"

"It's a saucepan."

"Yes, I know." Amusement bubbled through his words.

"Which is for making sauces. Cooking. Things like that." Cassidy slid her nail tip over the charred bottom. "In my experience, saucepans are more effective if you don't fossilize your meal in them. That way you can use them again."

He didn't respond. Instead he studied her with the lazy, relaxed manner of a man who had all the time in the world to lounge around. And he might well have.

She didn't.

But his silence offered Cassidy time to note his mussed jumble of almost-curls that framed a face made for the stubbled look. The Romanesque nose didn't diminish his appearance, nor did the dimples at the sides of his mouth. A faint scar on the edge of his chin only enhanced the chiseled jawline.

He was gorgeous.

But Cassidy wasn't here to admire handsome men. In fact, she would only be here long enough to work off her debt to Elizabeth Wisdom.

He crossed one long, lean leg over the other, stubbed a booted toe against a mark on the tile floor as if scraping one blob of scorched food from its filthy surface would make any difference.

Cassidy cleared her throat.

He lifted his head, blinked incredibly long lashes. Said nothing.

She raised her eyebrows expectantly.

His eyes danced, amused by her impatience.

"Tell you what. Since I belong here and you don't, perhaps you'd better tell me who you are."

Cassidy didn't think he belonged here. Not in a kitchen. Not in that white shirt—silk if she wasn't mistaken. The jacket—a designer brand for sure. Probably Italian.

No. He didn't look like he belonged in this mess.

But he *did* look like trouble.

The tall, rich and handsome kind of trouble.

"You do have a name, don't you?" he asked.

Add sense of humor to his assets.

"Of course I have a name. It's Cassidy." She tucked a lock of hair behind her left ear. "Cassidy Preston. Elizabeth Wisdom sent me. Apparently I'm to be the chef here for the next six months."

"You're the cook?" Sapphire deepened to impenetrable cobalt. The dimples vanished. He unfolded from his lazy stance and straightened. "Oh."

Not exactly the welcome she'd expected. He loomed over her, a few inches above six feet with perfect wide shoulders.

*Just right for a girl to tuck her head against.*

Not going to happen. A lying boss and a cheating fiancé had only reinforced what Cassidy had already learned from her father that men were not to be trusted.

No need for a refresher course.

"Ms. Preston?"

Even his voice was good-looking.

Cassidy blinked back to awareness, shook her head to silence her brain's warm hum. The straight-cut ends of her hair swung free, tickled her nose then fell right back into place against her jaw, which was exactly what she expected from her hairstyle. If only her life would work out that way.

Again, the man peered at her with that questioning stare, as if he'd said something and now awaited her response.

"Uh, yes, I'm the cook. Chef," she corrected. "Which is how I know saucepans need a little more care than this one's had. I'll need to use it. Preferably without charcoal."

He shook his head in mock reproof, eyes twinkling.

"We're not going to harp on a little burn, are we? At this rate, we'll never get anything done."

She cast a dubious glance at the mess surrounding them. "You've actually done something here?"

"Breakfast. Before that I was assessing." His left eye wrinkled into a rogue's wink while his lips curved upward in a lazy grin. He ambled toward her with the supreme confidence of a man fully in control of his universe. "It might not look difficult but it's really draining, trust me."

Trust him? Not with those daredevil eyes.

In spite of that resolution, Cassidy's breath logjammed as a whiff of his cologne tickled her nostrils. She'd always been a sucker for citrus. Ignoring this man was not going to be easy.

"Um—"

"I'm Tyson St. John. Ty to my friends. I am, or will be, the director of this place when it's up and running." He thrust out one hand, grasped hers. "I'm very pleased to meet you, Cassidy Preston. Will it cause you grief if I suggest the saucepan is beyond repair?"

The touch of his skin against hers ratcheted up Cassidy's respiration. Her knees turned to chicken noodle soup. Score ten for that killer smile.

Was this what they called charisma?

*He cannot be trusted.*

The warning that had carried her safely through the past popped up and jerked her back like a safety harness. She could not trust him.

Cassidy fought free of his magnetism. Why couldn't her new boss have been a sweet, chubby old man with bow legs and a face like a prune?

Her fingers tingled. She glanced down. Their hands were still melded together.

"Are you all right?"

Define *all right*. She had to survive six months of him. Judging by her overreaction, it wasn't going to be a cakewalk.

Dragging her fingers from his grip, Cassidy backed up two steps, inhaled a cleansing breath.

Cassidy completed a quick visual inspection of the room. "I don't know what to call this."

"Try chaos." An amused smile twisted his lips.

"Have you considered a cleaning service?"

"All part of my assessment." He waved a hand in front of his face, then coughed. "Besides a new kitchen, I guess we also need a new exhaust fan. That one sounds bad."

At last, something about which she could speak intelligently.

"They work better if they're clean. Most things do." Her brain took in what was there and its condition, ignoring the hot plate he'd used. "This place will need some refurbishment. Has the budget been set yet?"

"The Wisdom Foundation has been very generous." An infusion of starch altered his lazy manner. "This building wasn't cheap, but it's in the perfect location, and I think it's exactly what Gail would've wanted."

"Gail?"

The moment the word left her lips, his eyes froze. Tyson St. John didn't have to say a word. Any fool could guess from his reaction that Gail was someone special. His wife?

"I'm sorry. It's none of my business."

"Don't be. It's only—"After a moment's pause he grudgingly offered details. "Gail was the one with the view for this project—the Haven, that's what she wanted to call it." He tilted his head just the slightest degree, as if to hide his expression. "She saw it as a place where the hungry could come for a decent meal, where the homeless could find a bed and some warmth. A kind of community center."

"Well, there's certainly enough room to do all that in this old school. It's huge."

Tyson St. John remained silent while she navigated the

kitchen, opened sticky cupboard doors and peered into the dingy storeroom. He said nothing when she checked the interior of the ancient cooler and hastily backed away from the odor. He didn't even comment when she rattled the doors of the cast-iron monstrosity that had served as a stove in some previous lifetime.

Cassidy didn't say anything, either. But her heart sank faster than a stone thrown into Lake Michigan. It looked like nothing had changed since the building had been built. When she saw the narrow darkness of the receiving staircase she couldn't suppress a groan.

"What's wrong?"

"Transporting supplies up and down *that* will be a killer." She pushed open the door to an adjoining room and walked inside. Remnants of cafeteria tables and chairs lay all over the place.

"The dining room," he said from behind her, as if she hadn't already figured that out.

"Any idea how many people you expect to serve?"

Tyson St. John's shoulders went back. His brows drew together. He swallowed then shook his head.

"I'm, um, that is—er, I don't think we're that far yet. We only received possession of the property two months ago."

Two months? Surely his *assessing* should have been finished.

Frustration nipped at Cassidy's nerves, winching them a notch tighter. She'd expected to walk in here and get right to work, but with the kitchen not even ready to boil water, she foresaw her time extending exponentially.

"Mr. St. John—"

"Ty," he insisted.

"Ty. Since I'll only be here just six months," she emphasized softly, "I'd like to get to work as quickly as possible. Do you have a schedule for start-up?"

The welcome in those clear blue eyes frosted up. Goodbye sense of humor.

"We have a rough plan. My thought was that we would get your input before we made a decision on any big changes in the kitchen."

"My input." She seized the opportunity. "All right then. Do you have a pen?"

When he blinked Cassidy knew he wasn't prepared for her list. She'd give it to him anyway. They couldn't afford to waste time deciding who did what. January in Chicago was frigid and the homeless people would need a place to come to.

She removed her coat, pulled a black marker out of her purse, picked up a hunk of cardboard from the floor and laid it on the counter. As she wrote, she spoke.

"Most of the money will have to go toward the big-ticket items. Cooler, freezer. We'll need a new stove. I can manage with the pots and pans that are here. Now for small wares." She checked the cupboards, shrugged. "Not bad. I bring my own knives, so we can manage for now. I am going to need a mixer though."

She kept going, printing the things she needed—clearly and legibly so there would be no mistake about her requests.

"Wait!"

Cassidy froze at the barked order, peeked over one shoulder at her boss. His eyes gaped; he looked stunned.

Sympathy rose. She did tend to get carried away sometimes.

"Don't worry, I can adapt to minimal conditions. Now in regard to helpers—I'll need two. Full-time. Strong, willing to learn, not afraid of correction. It's important—"

"Ms. Preston, would you please stop?"

"Stop?"

"Yes. Stop." The relaxed demeanor had vanished, replaced by the deportment of a man used to giving orders.

The change in him made Cassidy catch her breath. Angry or teasing, he was still very good-looking, even when his eyes hardened to glacial chips and the steel in his voice warned her he wouldn't easily relinquish control.

"I realize you are a fully qualified chef, Ms. Preston, and that this must be a bit of a comedown for you. But the Haven is not—"

"Hey, Ty!" The yell was punctuated by the echo of an elephant herd tromping downstairs. A boy burst into the room. Well, not quite a boy. A preteen? "You'll never believe what I found."

Tyson St. John sighed as he raked a hand through his hair.

"No, I probably won't. Jack, this is Ms. Preston. She's a chef. Elizabeth Wisdom sent her to cook for us." His mouth tightened as he drew the boy forward. "This is my nephew, Ms. Preston. Meet Jackson Dorfman."

Cassidy found the introduction stilted, but had no time to dwell on it as Jack jerked away from the contact and frowned at her.

"A cook, huh? What kind?"

He was testing her. That belligerence, the bottom lip jutting out, the glare from those bittersweet brown eyes— all characteristic signs of onset teenager-hood. Two younger sisters had educated Cassidy in the challenges of that particular age very well. It was not an experience she yearned to repeat.

"It's nice to meet you, Jack." Cassidy met the glare head-on. "What kind of cook do you want?"

"I-I don't know." He seemed surprised by the question, not quite ready to back down, a bit curious. "You're not going to make things like liver pâté, are you? Or those things like clams that slide off slimy shells? Ty ordered them when we went for a fancy dinner one time."

She swallowed her laughter, kept her face straight. "Do you mean oysters?"

"Yeah, I guess. They were gross!"

Ty, good humor restored, winked at her before turning Jack to face him.

"I think I can safely assure you that Ms. Preston will not be offering oysters on her menu. Am I right?" he asked, glancing her way.

"I'm afraid so." She kept her face straight through a gargantuan effort. "At the Haven we will have to settle for things like beef stew, hot dogs, maybe some hamburgers. Once in a while, we might *have* to have roast beef, or maybe fried chicken. Unfortunately, I might even be forced to include pizza occasionally."

Out of the corner of her eye, Cassidy could see Ty's shoulders shake at her sad tone. She ignored him.

"That won't be too awful, will it, Jack?"

"Mom always said God answers prayer." Like lightning, the subject changed as Jack grabbed Ty's arm and yanked on it. "You've got to come see what I've found. It's the weirdest mirror. Come on!"

"Okay, okay, I'll be there in a minute." Ty shook his head at the burst of pounding footsteps overhead. "Remember, Jack," he called. "Be careful."

"Hurry!"

Cassidy was surprised by the soft look of yearning that washed over Tyson St. John's face as he gazed after his nephew, when just moments ago there had been stiffness in his attitude with the boy that she didn't understand.

"I'm really sorry Elizabeth didn't tell you that we aren't quite ready to open, Cassidy." Ty gnawed on his bottom lip. "I don't suppose you could get your boss to hire you back for a month or so, just until we get things shipshape?"

"I'd have to go back to Greece to do that and I don't think it would be worth it for one month." Cassidy kept her expression neutral as she surveyed the area. "I'll get settled in my place over the weekend. Monday morning I'll start cleaning in here. If you can find some helpers—"

A tremendous crash above them cut off the rest of her words. Ty instantly froze. One word whispered from his lips.

"Jack."

It took a second before he turned and raced out of the room, his footsteps hammering the stairs as he charged upward. Cassidy followed, besieged by memories. Ty paused on the first floor, but a weak cry from above them sent him racing up a second flight.

Ty charged through a doorway. Cassidy followed then jerked to a stop. Jack lay on his back by the far wall, shards of mirror surrounding his prone body, a pool of blood forming around his head. A six-inch jagged spear of glass protruded from his brow, barely missing his right eye.

"Oh, no." Ty remained frozen to the spot, hands clenching against his sides.

"Help me." Jack's words slipped from between lips drained so white they looked almost lifeless.

"Yes." But Ty's eyes brimmed with fear as they locked on Cassidy's, begging her to do something.

She slapped her phone into his palm before kneeling beside the injured boy.

"Call 911," she ordered. When he didn't obey, she snapped, "Now."

While he pushed the buttons, she did a quick survey of Jack then tried to make him more comfortable. A mirror hanging from the wall must have come off and landed on Jack.

"Lie still," she murmured. "You'll be fine. The ambulance will be here soon. It's going to be okay. Try not to move."

She felt Ty brush her arm as he crouched down beside her.

"They're coming. The glass—" he whispered. "Shouldn't we—" He reached out.

Cassidy grabbed his hand, pulled it back and held it with both of her own.

"Don't touch it!"

Jack's eyes flared open. She could see panic growing in their depths.

"Uncle Ty? Am I going to die like Mom?"

So he'd lost his mother. For a fraction of a moment, Cassidy could see into his boyish heart, to the uncertainty that lurked there like a monster in the night.

In that moment, a bond formed between them. She knew exactly how Jack felt because once, a long time ago, she'd felt the same. Scared, lonely, afraid that no one would ever love her as her dead mother had.

She released Ty's hand with a warning glance, then bent forward and placed her palms against Jack's cheeks. She waited till he was wholly focused on her.

"You're not going to die, Jack." She smiled to soften the harshness of her words, made her voice steady, reassuring. "You're going to lie very still until the paramedics come. They'll take you to the hospital and the doctors will help you. Then all the pretty nurses are going to come and fawn over you and offer you ice cream and try to get your telephone number for their daughters. Okay?"

Jack started to nod his head, but Cassidy tightened her fingers and held him still.

"You must have missed the first part," she teased. "Lie very still. Blink if you understand."

He blinked a whole bunch of times. Cassidy smiled.

"Good. I saw that in the movies and always wanted to try it." She grinned. "Guess it works, huh? Does your voice?"

"Yes."

"Thought so. Hey, that sounds like the ambulance." She turned to Ty. "Can you go and show them where to come?"

She knew from his expression that he did not want to leave. Yet something else told her that given the choice, Ty St. John would run as far and as fast from this situation as he could, which was exactly why she would not leave Jack. Ty was too upset to handle this.

When Ty opened his mouth to protest, Cassidy gave an almost imperceptible shake of her head and leaned so her lips were next to his ear.

"Go quickly."

He rose to his feet like a man in a daze, offered his nephew a shaky smile.

"I thought I was in charge here, but she's pretty bossy, don't you think?"

A smile fluttered across Jack's white lips. "Yeah."

"I think you and I are going to have to watch it. You keep your eye on her while I go get the paramedics." Tyson took one last look before hurrying out of the room.

Cassidy checked Jack's vitals, noted the widening circle of blood. She picked up his hand and held it between her own.

"You are doing fine, Jack."

"Can you pray for me?"

The words caught Cassidy off guard.

"When my mom was sick, she would ask me to pray for her. She always said it made her feel better. So can you pray for me?"

Years had passed since Cassidy had trusted anyone, let alone God. But Jack's pleading face could not be denied. She squeezed his hand and bowed her head, searching for the right words.

"God, you know that Jack has been hurt. And you know that he's afraid right now. Please help him."

It was a pathetic prayer, but at least it came to a quick end, thanks to the paramedics bursting into the room. She glanced down at Jack, felt the squeeze of his fingers around hers. One of the medics hunkered beside her, tried to nudge her out of the way. But Jack wouldn't let go of her hand.

"Thanks," he whispered, brown eyes shining.

"You're very welcome." Cassidy swallowed around the lump in her throat.

"Step back, please. We need to move him."

Jack squeezed her fingers once more, then let go. Cassidy stood by and watched them prepare him for the ride to the hospital.

Such gratefulness, and for what? A few paltry words? She had done nothing, and yet Jack seemed to relax, to gain confidence from her silly prayer. She watched as they loaded him onto a gurney, then followed as they carried him out of the building.

*A child's blind trust.* She'd had that once.

"I'm going with him. Would you be able to drive my car to the hospital?" Clearly back in control, Ty fished a set of keys out of the coat he was carrying. "It's parked behind the building. Ms. Preston?"

"Y-yes, of course." Cassidy gulped and accepted the keys from him. "I'll lock up and follow you. I want to see how he does, too."

Jack was inside the ambulance now. The paramedics waited impatiently, but Ty paused a moment longer, his face solemn.

"Thank you. I froze back there. I couldn't—" He shook his head as if to clear the image as he searched for words.

"Go." Cassidy urged him forward. "Your nephew needs you now."

He nodded, turned and strode toward the ambulance. Once he'd climbed inside, it took off. Shivering, she waited until the flashing lights disappeared from sight before turning back toward the building. Leaving Greece in January—was she crazy?

She retrieved her coat and purse, then stepped out the front door.

A grizzled old man, dressed in a shabby overcoat, stood on the bottom stoop.

"What happened?" He didn't sound like a curious on-looker. He sounded concerned, worried.

She debated whether or not to tell him, then decided it could do no harm. But first she had some questions of her own.

"Who are you?"

"Mac. I've been coming here awhile, helping Ty get the place cleaned out." The skin on his forehead drew into a crease. "The boy got hurt, didn't he?"

"Yes, Jack broke a mirror and some of it cut him. He's going to need some stitches. I'm going to the hospital as soon as I lock up."

"Ty'll blame himself."

"It wasn't his fault. It was an accident."

"Ty doesn't always see things that way."

That sounded strange but Cassidy had no time to probe deeper. She stepped around him, pulled the door closed and used the keys Elizabeth had sent her to lock it.

"Things will probably be back to normal on Monday. Why don't you come back then."

He nodded, turned away. "Ty will have nightmares tonight."

Cassidy frowned as she watched him leave. Ty? Nightmares? What an odd thing to say. Maybe he'd meant Jack.

As Cassidy drove to the hospital, her thoughts flew to the young boy who'd lost so much blood and to the man who'd seemed more traumatized than the child.

Not that it was any of her business.

But when she weighed her own electric connection with Tyson St. John with the unusual way his nephew had touched something she usually kept buried deep inside, Cassidy couldn't help being intrigued by Ty and Jack's relationship.

*You're here to do a job and not to get sidetracked by a good-looking man and his nephew.*

Her brain issued the message, but it also conjured up an image of Ty leaning against the counter, winking at her. Her pulse fluttered in response.

*Don't even go there. Focus on your future.*

And the dream.

Yeah, she'd concentrate on the dream.

# Chapter Two

Cassidy Preston was late.

Ty tossed two more bags of garbage into a plastic bin, then glanced—for the tenth time—at the big metal clock on the kitchen wall.

"Seems like the cook must've slept in, Elizabeth," he muttered as he swept up a pile of debris. "How is she going to handle breakfast at six if she can't get to work on a Monday morning by eleven?"

"You might be surprised by what I can handle."

Ty whirled around. Cassidy leaned against the door frame, wearing a short espresso-toned jacket shot with the same silver as her eyes. Her smug expression told him she hadn't been sleeping in. He was stupidly pleased by the way her eyes lit up when she looked around.

"Very nice." Her gaze rested for a moment on the saucepan he'd left on the counter—the sparkling clean saucepan. A smile eased the severity of her lips. "I hear Jack was released. Everything okay?"

"He's doing very well. Thanks for asking. The doctors sent him home once they were sure he was okay and the stitches were holding. He's supposed to be on bed rest till school starts, but I doubt anyone can hold him to that." Ty grimaced. "Keeping him quiet while he heals is going to be the hard part."

"Well, he *is* a boy. I don't suppose it's all that easy to lie around when all your friends are outside."

Ty could've told her that Jack didn't have many friends, that ever since his mother's death he'd grown more introverted. He could've told her that he was concerned by the boy's aimlessness, by his lack of interest in the swimming team on which he'd once excelled, or the Rollerblading that had worried his mother. He could've told her that, since Gail's death, he'd tried a thousand things to draw the boy's interest and that none of them had worked.

Thankfully, he didn't get a chance to relate that sad history.

"You've made quite a difference in here. Did you work all weekend?"

"Nope. I started at the crack of dawn." No way would he tell her why. "Someone tried to break in Friday night so I hired Mac to act as our night watchman. He was a cop once. He says you've met."

She nodded.

"When I showed up here this morning it was pretty early. I think I scared the wits out of him." The old man's disgruntled complaints still rang in Ty's ears.

"Well, whenever you started and however long it took, you've done a great job."

"Thank you. Does that mean you're cooking lunch?"

She tossed him a "when pigs fly" look.

"Regarding that." Cassidy frowned. "I wonder if it would be possible to haul out those old refrigeration units while you're in your cleaning mode. They smell."

"Haul them away?" Did he look like an ox? "Sure—if I

can scrounge up about another six men and some kind of pulley system."

"I can help you." She took another look, shaking her head. "You're right. We'd need Hercules."

Ty probed past the friendly smile, glimpsed something she wasn't saying.

"These old things are all we have. If we throw them out—"

A satisfied smirk originated in Cassidy's silver-gray eyes and swooped down to tip up the corners of her generous mouth. Funny he hadn't noticed her great smile before, but then she hadn't smiled all that much on Friday.

"They *were* all you had." A spark of mischief played with her smile. "I found something better."

"You bought new refrigeration?" he asked in disbelief, temper rising at her temerity. He tamped it down with difficulty. "Cassidy, there is no way we can lay out expenditures like that without sourcing all possible providers and getting quotes for the best price. I know you want to get started but you can't rush ahead on your own."

"If you'd only—"

"Wherever you got it from, it will have to go back. I'm sorry." Ty pinned her with a glare, hoping she understood what he wasn't saying—he was the boss. "You have to take it back."

"Could you listen—"

"I don't have to hear any more. It goes back."

Ty was in charge so she'd better realize *he* would make the major decisions about where the money was spent. He could be more blunt if he had to, but confrontation wasn't his usual style.

Apparently their new chef had no such problem.

"How dare you?"

Silver flashes from her eyes speared him. So she had a temper. Well, he wasn't any pushover, either.

"There is no dare about it," Ty informed her with a firmness that, thanks to Jack, he'd recently learned to apply. "Elizabeth Wisdom's foundation donated money to turn Gail's dream into reality. But I can't authorize—"

"Stop!" She took one step toward him, anger shimmering around her like a field of overcharged electricity. Her voice had risen but her next words were modulated. "I realize you're in charge here, Mr. St. John. I'm well aware that everything must be approved by you. You are the boss. Got that."

"Then?" He would not back down.

"I have no intention of threatening your power. I was merely trying to help get this place off the ground. As quickly as possible."

"But—"

Cassidy's upheld palm stemmed his protest.

"That's why I contacted a friend of mine—to get a lead on some equipment. Davis was willing to donate some very good units for which he has no further use."

His anger shrank to the size of a shriveled pea. "Donate?"

"As in *free.* Gratis. No charge." She glanced at her watch for the second time. "They'll be delivered in about two hours. Also free. If we have everything ready, they might just agree to move the units into place."

Ty had jumped to conclusions, neglecting to ask questions first. In short, he'd done exactly what he always counseled his patients *not* to do. Like some power-hungry freak that sensed his control was threatened, he'd waved his big stick of authority to prove to her that he knew what he was doing.

"I'm sorry."

It wasn't much of an apology, but at least it was sincere. Ty stared at his toes, waiting for her response. What happened now would signal how their relationship progressed. Yes, he'd messed up, but they still had to work together.

She could have called, he told himself, and alerted him to

the possibility that she'd found some equipment. She could have mentioned she was going to ask some friends for help. She could have—

Ty didn't have time to analyze his defensiveness.

"Clearly, I made a mistake. You don't want them." Cassidy shoved a length of hair behind one ear. "Fine. I'll phone Davis, see if he will take it all back. I didn't realize that you had something else already planned. I got so excited when this was available for free that I guess I thought—" She heaved a sigh, closed her eyes and shook her head. "Never mind. I'm sorry I interfered with your plans."

Now he felt like a first-class jerk.

"I didn't actually have any plans. Yet. I'm very happy you found this opportunity for us, Cassidy." Ty caught himself waiting for the glow to return to her face.

"You're sure?" Who could blame her for being confused?

"Positive." He took a deep breath and said what he should have said in the first place. "In case you haven't noticed, I'm a little awed by the responsibility of getting this place up and running. My sister, Gail—" he struggled to find the right words "—she had a very precise idea of what she wanted the Haven to be like. She spent a lot of time working in this community as an outreach worker. She chose this place because our brother died near here."

"I'm sorry. I didn't know."

"You couldn't have. As much as I can, I intend to make her dream come true, preferably without spending all the money Elizabeth provided us before we open the doors. Most of the time I'm in way over my head, just trying to stay afloat. And it scares me to death. I guess I took my fears out on you." Forcing that admission cost Ty but he pressed on. "I sincerely apologize."

Cassidy's body language told Ty she wasn't ready to accept his apology quite yet. He tried again.

"If it seems like I'm a little overprotective about the place, it's probably because I am. Organizing a shelter—" He held out his hands, palms facing upward. "It's not my area of expertise and I don't want to make any mistakes. I'm feeling my way through."

"What is your field?"

"Counseling. I'm a psychologist. I used to work in the military with the soldiers serving in Iraq."

"You don't now?" Curiosity lit up her expression. "Why is that?"

"I quit." He struggled to find words that would make sense of a situation that even now confused him. "Shortly after I came back, Gail had a massive coronary."

At first he'd considered coming here charity work, but the longer he concentrated on the Haven, the more Ty began to imagine Gail's vision coming alive for the residents of this neighborhood—for people like Donnie, who had fallen through the cracks.

In running the Haven Ty saw himself finding his way back to counseling, to helping people improve their lives, work he'd loved.

At least that was his hope.

The truth was that he'd latched onto the Haven like a life preserver because he never again wanted to relive the gut-wrenching horrors he'd seen, terrors he still dreamed of every night.

And of course there was Jack. Ty hoped seeing his mother's dream come true would help Jack get past the grief that still showed in his eyes, help the two of them bond.

But that wasn't the entire truth.

In reality, Ty desperately needed the myriad details of this place to keep from panicking about raising a twelve-year-old boy alone.

"Losing your sister must have been devastating, both to you

and to Jack," Cassidy murmured. "Especially for you, having also lost your brother. I'm so sorry."

That she could be so considerate, especially after his temper tantrum, touched Ty.

"Thank you. It was difficult. But knowing her vision for the Haven is going to become real—that helps a lot."

"Would you mind telling me what that vision was? How it started?"

Ty closed his eyes, raked a hand through his hair as loss squeezed a grip around his heart.

"Gail and Elizabeth Wisdom were friends for years. They sat on lots of charity boards together."

In fact, it was Gail who'd introduced Ty to Elizabeth. He recalled the Christmas benefit as if it were yesterday. He'd attended just before he'd been shipped out and found himself caught up in their projects, in the joy they took lending help where it was needed. Those had been happy days.

Later Ty had been glad of the connection when he'd contacted the Wisdom Foundation about making Gail's dream come true.

"The two of them were like twin caped-crusaders, hunting for things that needed to be done to make the world a better place, and tackling them till they got the results they were after." He shook his head ruefully. "The Haven grew from an idea Gail had at her last high school reunion. Our brother died of a drug overdose in his senior year. When Gail found out this school was going to be demolished, she decided to use it to make this neighborhood better for the people who live here."

"She sounds very generous."

Good thing Jack wasn't here. Ty longed to talk about his sister, but since Jack hadn't yet opened up about losing his mother, Ty wasn't sure exactly how to broach the subject. So he kept silent, never speaking about the sister he'd loved, allowing Jack time to deal with his grief in his own way.

Someday he hoped to share all the funny stories from his childhood. Someday he'd pull out the old photos, talk to Jack about Donnie, how he'd gotten messed up because he made the wrong choices. Someday Ty and Jack would laugh, push past the strained relationship they now shared.

"I'm sorry if it's painful—"

Ty shook his head.

"Gail had a very successful career in real estate. She left it to work in this community as an outreach worker because she felt that God had blessed her so much she had to share, to make a difference in the world. And for several years she did."

"I see."

Ty breathed deeply, forced his shoulders to relax and his fingers to unclench.

"The Haven was Gail's last dream. I made myself a promise that I'd see my sister's final project through to completion."

Silence stretched between them for several moments. Ty felt Cassidy's gray gaze studying him but he kept his head down, his focus on the floor, because he didn't want her to see how much that promise was costing him.

Nobody knew of his long nights lying awake, trying to recall if he'd dotted all the i's, crossed all the t's, missed any detail that would jeopardize the project. That's why he didn't go to bed till long after midnight. That's why he'd been up at four this morning.

Well, one reason why.

He spent precious hours deliberating over every decision, desperate to avoid the mistake that would spoil Gail's dream. But even when he finally made a choice, Ty could never be sure it was the right one. That and the constant nightmares were just a small part of the legacy post-traumatic stress disorder had bequeathed him—chronic worry and uncertainty. PTSD was the primary reason he'd left the military, left counseling to someone else, someone who wasn't dragging about his baggage.

Eventually he hoped to ease back into practice in his own way, on his own terms. Elizabeth had been great with her advice and support, her foundation equally generous, but even she didn't know exactly how much he had at stake. Whether he could recover, whether he could listen and help someone else—what he discovered here would decide whether he ever practiced again.

For now Ty would see the Haven through to completion—errors and all.

What happened after that—Ty didn't want to think about it right now.

"May I say something?"

He'd almost forgotten she was there. Cassidy waited until he lifted his head and looked at her.

"I am not trying to usurp your authority, Ty. I don't want to get in your way, change your decisions or mess with your plans. That is not my intent." She stood straight and tall, unflinching in her vivid sweater and frayed but fitted jeans. "I am here to help for six months. I owe that to Elizabeth because six years ago she gave me back my life. But at the end of my six months I'll go my own way, get on with my own plans."

"Okay." *Gave her back her life?* There was more to that story, but Cassidy didn't look inclined to explain at the moment.

Ty's curiosity grew. That was the second time she had emphasized that she was here for six months. Had she repeated it for his benefit, or for her own?

"Until then, please know that I'll do my very best to help you make the Haven succeed."

"Thank you. I appreciate your commitment."

"I *am* committed. From now on I promise not to spring any further surprises on you. I'm sure you're juggling a thousand things already. You don't need me adding to your stress." She offered a tentative smile. "All right?"

Ty shook his head.

"Not all right at all. Please don't apologize for helping. This whole misunderstanding was my fault. For now, let's agree that we will cooperate to make things go smoothly. The Haven is our common goal. Okay?"

"Very okay." She glanced around the room. Suddenly her eyes opened wide. She gasped. "Oh, how silly. I forgot."

"Forgot who?"

"Not who, what."

Ty followed her pointing finger and saw two brown paper cups sitting on the table by the door she'd entered. Next to them she'd left a white bag with his favorite bakery's red logo printed across it.

"Those." She handed him a cup. "I hope it's not cold yet."

"You've been back in Chicago what—five days? And you've already found Sugar's?" Ty sniffed the aromatic wisps emanating from the tiny opening in the lid. "Costa Rican. Double dark, twice ground with real cream."

Her eyebrows lifted. "I take it you're familiar with that brew."

"You could say that." He closed his eyes, inhaled and sighed. "This is going to be a very good day."

"I should have given you the coffee first."

The way she said it made him study her. A tiny smile kicked up the corner of her pretty mouth; her eyes sparkled as if enjoying a private joke.

"Because?"

"We could have avoided a lot of misunderstanding if I'd known one cup would mellow you out for the whole day."

"Okay, probably not the whole day," Ty admitted. "But it's a very good start. Thank you." He sipped the drink and allowed himself a moment to savor it. A crackling bag drew him back to the reality of the Haven's less than immaculate kitchen.

"I suppose you're not into apple Danish?" She held out one of his favorite delicacies. When he didn't immediately take it, she shrugged. "That's okay. I'm starved. I bought four thinking I'd have one for breakfast, one for lunch and share the other two. Guess I'll keep some for tomorrow."

"I don't see any need for you to suffer like that." Ty plucked the golden pastry from her fingertips. "I'm happy to help out." He bit into it quickly, so she couldn't snatch it back, then faked wide-eyed innocence. "Oh, I'm sorry. Am I eating yours?"

Ty's mouth watered. He'd missed breakfast, and dinner the night before was a faint memory of peanut butter and dill pickles. Jack's favorite. They made a decent sandwich if you were starving, but only just.

"You don't look very sorry."

"I truly am." He held the uneaten portion toward her assuming his saddest look.

"Nice gesture." She took a tiny bite, laughed at him. "You don't do pathetic well, you do know that?"

Ty gave it a second effort but she merely shook her head.

"Forget it. I prefer apricots, anyway."

"You have apricot Danish, too? That's another favorite of mine." He enjoyed watching laughter change her face. "Yours has more icing."

"Tough." She took another bite, displaying not the least hint of regret.

"As your boss, I feel compelled to say—"

"Thank you, Cassidy. You've saved my life. Again." She tilted her head sideways in a sassy fashion. "That *was* what you were going to say, wasn't it?"

"Sort of."

"There's a guy outside—hey, nobody said anything about

food. I love Danish." Mac glanced back and forth between the two of them like a puppy who doesn't know which benefactor to attack first.

"That must be Davis." Cassidy dabbed her lips with a napkin and held out the bag. "We meet again, Mac. Help yourself. There's plenty." She grabbed her coat.

"Maybe you should wait to sample the goodies till later, Mac." Ty eyed the pastry bag, licked his lips. "At least until we see what Cassidy's friends have brought us."

"Until you get your gums around it, you mean. No way." Mac chose his Danish and carried it with him as he followed them upstairs, smacking his lips to taunt Ty.

Ty pulled on his jacket thinking how Mac accepted everyone at face value. But Ty had a thousand questions about their chef.

Was she married? Why had she left Europe? Did she have any family?

"Tyson St. John, meet my friend Chef Davis Longfellow. Davis, Mac."

This guy was a chef? He looked like a wrestler and it had nothing to do with the thick down coat he wore. Ty exchanged greetings before the gigantic stainless-steel units lying on the flatbed attached to a half-ton grabbed his attention. They looked like they'd require a crane to lift them off.

"Thank you so much for the donation, Davis," he said, meaning it. "It's very generous of you. The Haven will put them to good use."

"Then that's thanks enough." Davis hopped on the back of the flatbed and began undoing the ropes that secured the units. "God sure moved in a timely fashion on this."

"Why do you say that?" Ty applied himself to untying a second set of ropes at the back of the truck, jumped when Davis's laugh burst out like a clap of thunder.

"'Why?' he asks. Let's see, I've been waiting for my new

refrigeration units for close to six months. Last week the vendor called to say they had been lost in shipping, that they couldn't supply for another eight weeks at best."

"Bad news."

"It was, until last night. After the dinner rush, I got a call. The truck had mysteriously arrived in town. It was on a rush order, and if we couldn't get my stuff unloaded right away I'd have to wait till they were able to come back around—some time next week, while I'm on vacation." He tossed the rope free, gave Ty a questioning look.

"Okay," Ty agreed. "That does sound like God put in some overtime."

"It gets better. Two minutes after I got off the phone, Cassidy wandered in to say hello and mentioned she was looking for used equipment. If that isn't God working, I don't know what is."

"Well, it's certainly our good fortune." Cassidy picked up the ropes and set them in a neat pile beside the walk.

"Oh, Cass, you doubter!" Davis shook his head in disgust and hopped down. "Good fortune, nothing. It's perfect planning by the Father and you know it."

"It's chance."

"Chance?" He hooted with derision, winked at Ty. "How's this for chance? If that stuff had come while I was away I would've had to come back and my family would not have liked that. At all."

"That doesn't mean—"

Ty didn't understand why she'd grown so annoyed.

"If it had come tomorrow morning, I would've missed the plane we are supposed to catch—the one with nonrefundable tickets to sun and surf. If I'd had to wait another eight weeks, the repairs they're doing on the building would've had to be put off." Davis waggled a finger at her. "As I said, God at work."

"I think you're right." Ty smiled at him.

"You guys always stick together." Belligerence colored Cassidy's voice.

"I have some repairs planned for around here, too. Moving this stuff in after they're completed wouldn't have been easy," Ty added. He wished Jack had shoveled off all the walks when he'd been asked. Now patches of ice had formed making the sidewalks treacherous.

"Your boss agrees with me, Cass. Divine Providence at work for both the giver and the receiver. How can you still doubt?"

Cassidy's pretty face hardened into rigid lines. "Believe what you want," she snapped, chin lifting.

Puzzled by her reaction, Ty walked around the flatbed, studying it from many different angles.

"How exactly do we get these beasts inside?" he finally asked.

*"Many hands make light work."*

"Davis is big on these homilies." Cassidy's eyes danced with glee. "Actually, Davis is just plain big."

"Ha. Cassidy is too funny today." Her friend didn't seem to take offense. "Move out of the way, you puny woman. We men have to work." He flexed his bicep then leaned his head toward Ty. "See the way her eyebrow twitches. That means she's steamed and she's thinking up ways to pay us back."

"Thanks for the warning." Judging by the glares the two were exchanging, Ty guessed they'd known each other for quite a while. "Forewarned is forearmed."

"Don't you start." Cassidy yanked hard on a bit of leftover rope. "I thought you said you're getting ready for a vacation, Davis. It's cold out here. Don't you have something to do other than stand around and jabber?"

"Tsk tsk. I hoped Europe would have cured you of that crankiness." Davis pulled out a cell phone and began dialing. "If I can just figure out where my 'many hands' are, I will prove how much truth there is in my little homily."

He hadn't completed punching in the last number before a big black truck pulled up to the curb and four muscled men jumped out.

"About time you got here." Davis introduced them to Ty.

Once they'd greeted him, the men took turns wrapping Cassidy in a bear hug, swinging her around, then planting a loud kiss on her cheek. By the time they were finished her face glowed and she giggled like a young girl. Ty couldn't stop staring at her.

"Good to see you again, Cass."

"Good to see you, too, I think." When they lunged toward her again, Cassidy stepped backward and pointed to the flatbed. "Could we get some work done here today? It's supposed to snow again, you know."

The four men glanced at Davis. "Hasn't changed much, has she?"

"Nope. Just as bossy as she ever was."

Cassidy snorted her disgust while the four pulled a cart from the truck's bed and handed it up to Davis, who began fastening it to the first piece of machinery. Obviously they knew what they were doing, so Ty followed their directions and did exactly as he was told. A little better than half an hour later, both units were installed and running nicely. The old ones had been removed and were now tied onto the flatbed.

He overheard Cassidy promising to repay the five men with her specialty, which sounded chocolaty and very fattening.

"You going to provide shelter here, too, like with beds and everything?" Crank, the man with the biggest biceps, insisted Ty give them a tour of the old school building.

"That's the idea. It's a bit much for us to do all at once so I guess we'll start with a soup kitchen and work up from there. Want to see more?"

"Yes."

Ty led them through the building. Eventually they came to the gym. "This is the best part."

"No kidding." Hart, the tallest of the four men, grabbed a basketball from a box in the corner, raced across the floor and sank a hoop shot.

"You haven't lost your touch." Cassidy lounged in the doorway, watching them. "This old school has a big playground. Come spring, you guys could spend a day putting up a fort, some swings, maybe a few slides. Couldn't you?"

"Could," Hart agreed.

Ty couldn't help staring. He hadn't imagined Cassidy had given any thought to the Haven, let alone considered future possibilities.

Furtive whispers drew him back to awareness. Cassidy nodded at Crank, who seemed tongue-tied.

"He's willing to donate some bedsprings from a motel he just bought."

"Great." Feeling as if he'd been grasped by one of those muscled arms and shaken, Ty gulped. But before he could accept, she continued.

"Hart's brother's a football pro. He could get some gym equipment for you."

"Not fancy, but free," Hart inserted.

"It's really kind of you, all of you."

Apparently his message about being in charge hadn't sunk in at all. But Ty didn't mind when Cassidy took over, coaxing Davis to approach his church for donations toward a day care, mocking his upturned nose.

"What's the matter, Davis?" Cassidy teased. "Not into diapers?"

"Funny." He ignored her to face Ty. "Her humor hasn't changed since we were in high school together. It's still nonexistent."

"High school?" Ty recalled the way she'd interacted with the other men. "All of you?"

"Afraid so." Davis laughed at Cassidy's groan. He leaned toward Ty and spoke sotto voce. "Cassidy was number one on everybody's dating list."

"Liar. I never made it onto anyone's dating list." She thumped Davis on the shoulder. "You never even knew I was alive until you discovered I could cook." She glanced at Ty. "They had some kind of contest to see who would persuade me to go out with them first."

"I won." Davis thrust out his massive chest.

"You won because you conned me." Her scathing tones dared him to deny it. "Anyway, that wasn't a date. You got me to cook a meal under the pretext of helping your poor sick mother."

"He said you offered because you were infatuated with him."

"You actually believed that?" Cassidy rolled her eyes.

Crank made a threatening gesture at Davis. "Your past is coming back to haunt you big-time now that Cass is back. You know what she's like about lying."

"Hates it. Yeah, I know that." Davis sobered immediately. "I'm sorry, Cass."

Ty found her reaction curious. His first impression of the chef had been of a strong, aggressive and capable woman. Somehow he never imagined her as an uncertain high school girl trying to figure out the intricacies of dating. Seeing her interaction with these men added a sense of vulnerability, made her more approachable.

"You're going to be very sorry you lied about me, Davis." Cassidy's words held a thin edge of pain. A moment later her grin flashed. "I'm going to think up some really big payback."

"Look, forget the past. I'm more interested in the present."

"I'm sure you are." Cassidy winked at Ty then turned to

face her friend. "I could tell a lot of stories on you, Davis, and you know it. But because you came through today, I won't."

Relief washed over the big man's face.

"And because you got me interested in cooking and pushed me to get my own place, I guess I owe you one, too." He risked a look over one shoulder. Crank and his friends were huddled together, muttering about a football game on the weekend. Davis ignored them, turned to face Ty. "So it's okay with you, if I suggest your place as a project for our church?"

"I'll be very thankful for anything your church is willing to help us with." Ty glanced at the others. "That goes for all of you. The Haven is only going to work if we get community support. Then people will see we are only trying to help. Hopefully that will allay any suspicions that are out there."

"That sounds like you have problems." Cassidy frowned at him.

"Some local kids have made a few threats. Nothing we can't handle." Ty hoped that was true.

"You're welcome to join us at our church if you like, Ty. First Street Community Church isn't big, but it's all heart. We would welcome you anytime."

Since Ty had been thinking about finding a permanent church home for himself and Jack since they'd moved, he listened to Davis's directions.

"If I can persuade my nephew, you might just see us there on Sunday. And you must feel free to come here anytime—all of you. As soon as I get a coffeepot working there will be a cup for you whenever you like."

"Thanks."

Each man shook Ty's hand, teased Cassidy, then clambered up the steps. Except for Davis. He lingered behind while the others called for Cassidy and Mac to come and see something on the big black truck they'd arrived in. She gave the two of them a speculative look before following the others outside.

Ty walked up the stairs beside Davis wondering what the other man was struggling to say.

"So you and Cassidy are both chefs," he prodded. "That's interesting."

"Technically I'm a chef, but I'm not in Cassidy's league." The big man shrugged. "She's won about every award they give, made her mark with the best in the business. She could work anywhere and they'd be more than happy to have her."

"Yet she chose to come back to Chicago." Ty wanted to hear more about Cassidy Preston. Particularly why she was so adamant about not overstaying her six-month term.

"She always had big plans for her future."

Something in Davis's voice made Ty pause just outside the door, while they were still out of earshot of the others.

"You don't think her future is why she came back?"

"I didn't say that."

Ty met his look, smiled faintly. "You didn't have to."

"Psychologist, huh?" Davis shook his head. "I'll have to watch it."

"You going to hang around here all afternoon, Davis?" Hart bellowed. "Or do you want help unloading that stuff?"

"I want help, of course. Think the Haven might get a few bucks for the metal if we take it over to that friend of yours?"

"Why not?"

Moments later the men and the old equipment had disappeared down the snowy street.

"Not a bad morning's work," Cassidy said as she turned to go back inside.

Ty grasped her arm. "Wait a minute."

She glanced at his hand, eyes steely as she waited for him to release her. Then she lifted her gaze to meet his. "Yes?"

"It's past noon," he said, checking his watch. "I'm hungry."

"Oh. Okay. Well, have a nice lunch."

Ty stepped in front of the door so she couldn't go inside. She lifted her perfectly arched eyebrows to glare at him. "Excuse me?"

He laughed.

"I can see I'm going to have to practice my communication skills. That was supposed to have been an invitation for lunch. I'm buying. As a thank-you," he explained. "Getting that equipment, bringing those men here, listening to their offers to help—if they pan out, the place will have taken a giant leap forward. Thanks to you."

"You're welcome." It was a duty response carrying little emotion.

Ty tried again.

"So what do you say we take a break over lunch and you can tell me what other things you see happening at the Haven?"

For the first time since Ty had met her, Cassidy Preston was speechless.

He waited, shuffling from one foot to the other until, exasperated by her lack of response, he burst out, "I'd appreciate a decision soon. I do have some work to do this afternoon."

Her laughter bounced off the building and down the street.

"I think, counselor, that you need a refresher in patience."

"What I need is an answer. Lunch?"

She studied him for a few moments, her expression unreadable. He was about to give up when she nodded, once.

"I guess we could take a break. For an hour or so."

Within ten minutes she was seated in the front seat of his car and Ty was trying to figure out how Cassidy Preston could be so animated when some old high school buddies showed up, yet turn into a marble statue when they were alone.

As he pulled into the parking lot of a restaurant, Ty saw her check her watch for the third time.

Apparently he had about as long as it took to order and eat lunch to find the answer to his questions.

## Chapter Three

"Would it help if I apologized again?"

Cassidy winced as her fork clattered against the plate. She left it there, hid her hands in her lap and tried to figure out what Tyson St. John had been talking about.

"I mean, I could if it would help." He'd finished his meal already. "I know I jumped on you about the refrigeration and I truly am sorry, but—"

"Please, it's fine. I understand that you've been under some stress. Really, there's no problem." She let their server take away her spinach salad even though she'd only tasted about three bites. "I'm just glad we have what we need and that we can move on."

"Davis mentioned something about you living in Europe. Were you there long?"

She knew where the questions were leading. Not that there was anything wrong with them. Ty was only interested. But that didn't make opening up any easier.

She didn't know where to start.

Ty folded his napkin, laid it to one side.

"Forget I asked. I can take you back now, if you want." His

voice had lost the soft lilt she had admired earlier. Now it was flat, emotionless.

Cassidy swallowed. They had to work together for the next six months. No matter how raw coming back made her feel, remaining silent was a lousy way to start off a working relationship.

"Actually I was away for six years. Elizabeth Wisdom's foundation gave me a scholarship to start my training in Paris. After that I worked with some of the best chefs in the world. I guess I've moved around quite a bit compared to some people. But I've enjoyed it."

"So coming back here wasn't exactly what you wanted?" He insisted she choose dessert and asked for coffee. "Chicago doesn't feel like home anymore?"

Cassidy tasted a tiny morsel of her cheesecake before setting down her fork.

"It isn't that. I grew up in Chicago. I have a lot of fond memories of this place."

"And some not-so-fond ones, judging by your expression just now." His intent scrutiny pushed past her barriers. "Do you want to talk about them? I've been told I'm a good listener."

*Talk about them?* Cassidy never wanted to even think about the past again. So she did what she always did, drew the focus away from herself.

"I have two sisters. One lives in the city and one lives about forty miles away. It's nice to be close to them again." She sipped her water, licked her lips and stalled for time.

"I'm sure it is. No parents?"

"No."

Silence yawned. It was obvious Ty was not going to press for more information, which Cassidy found reassuring.

"What about you?" she challenged. "You gave up your

career and now you're building your sister's dream. What does your family think of that?"

Ty shook his head, a rueful smile touching the corners of his mouth.

"Since I don't have one, I don't have to worry."

"Except for Jack, of course."

An odd look washed across his face before he mumbled, "Yes, Jack."

He didn't want to discuss his life any more than she did, so Cassidy filled in the rest of the time with small talk and amusing stories about some of her cooking trials. By the time she'd coaxed him into eating most of her cheesecake, she felt more relaxed. By the look on the Ty's face, he did, too.

On the way back to the car Cassidy got down to business.

"Can you give me some idea of when you expect me to start producing meals?"

"I can't really. I'm not sure exactly what else I need to get in place before we open our doors. Unofficially, of course."

"Oh." Meaning he was going to keep assessing?

"I'm hoping we can have most of our programs running before we hold our grand opening." He laughed as he pulled open her door. "But that's a long way into the future."

"Not that long, I hope." She sank into the car seat wondering if it was only uncertainty that made him take so long to get things done. Or did something else underlie his hesitation?

"Let's give ourselves a few days to assess." There was a tone of finality in the words.

When they arrived at the Haven, Elizabeth Wisdom was deep in conversation with Mac, who seemed quite at home with the elegant heiress from Texas.

"Hello, Cassidy," Elizabeth greeted, hugging her. "You look very well. And Ty. I'm so sorry about Jack. He's recovering?" She linked her arms in theirs and walked between them into the building.

"Jack will be fine. I'm very glad Cassidy was there." His voice altered. "The sight of all that blood got to me and I froze."

Elizabeth's gentle smile sympathized.

"Poor Ty. How did you manage in the army hospital?"

Cassidy had wondered the same thing.

"I'm a psychologist. I didn't have anything to do with the medical side. Never even had to use my first-aid knowledge."

"Well, that will probably change as renovations begin, so you'd better toughen up." Elizabeth patted his shoulder in a motherly way, then turned to Cassidy. "And you, my dear. I hear you've been busy replacing kitchen equipment since your plane landed last Thursday. Bravo. Is your accommodation suitable?"

"The house is lovely, Elizabeth, thank you."

"I know it's tiny—"

"It's perfect for one person," Cassidy assured her, secretly delighted to have a house all to herself. "The big south windows are perfect to grow my herbs. I don't need anything more. After all, it's only for six months."

"Yes." Elizabeth's smooth alabaster forehead pleated for a moment then smoothed. "We must make hay while the sun shines. That's what my father used to say, though he never made any hay. He far preferred oil." She stopped, surveyed the interior hall and frowned. "This is too grim."

Cassidy remained silent, watching as Ty shot down every one of Elizabeth's suggestions for renovation. He claimed he wanted the Haven to be a great success, a tribute to his sister, and yet, as they moved through the building, Ty stalled and stumbled when called upon to clarify his ideas. By the time they reached the kitchen, he seemed relieved that the focus was off him and on her.

"My dear, you did very well to find these," Elizabeth congratulated. "What else have you planned?"

Cassidy set out her ideas clearly and concisely but even here Ty didn't seem able to concentrate. He got stuck on details, rattled on about how the Haven's outreach shouldn't begin until they were sure of their focus and their target group. Cassidy grew so frustrated she got up and left, just to get a breather. She returned with a teakettle, some cookies and a box of teabags.

Ty didn't appear to notice she'd been absent until she set the teapot before Elizabeth. Then he simply looked puzzled; he left his sentence hanging unfinished.

Something was clearly wrong, but what? He'd said he was nervous about making a mistake. Maybe that explained all the barricades he was erecting.

"I thought we could all use a break," Cassidy said.

"What a lovely idea." Elizabeth poured the thick amber liquid into the three mugs Cassidy had scrubbed spotless.

"I didn't know we had a kettle here." Ty added sugar to his tea, frowned then shook his head. "You bought one?"

Cassidy shrugged. "My gift to the kitchen."

Ty opened his mouth as if to protest, but obviously had second thoughts. He shrugged and smiled, lifted his cup.

"To the Haven."

They clinked mugs together. Elizabeth glanced around the messy room, her face expressing her distaste, though she didn't give it voice.

"Next steps for you, Cassidy?" Elizabeth pulled out a small notebook.

"Arrange suppliers, find some helpers and generally plan how this will work. I'll do two test runs. One on Thursday at noon to feed whoever is working here." She looked at Ty. "If you can let me know approximately how many workers will be here, it will help me prepare."

"Sure."

She read his expression clearly.

*Exactly how am I supposed to know that?*

"Maybe you could count heads around nine. Or I could." Cassidy struggled for a less bossy tone but it wasn't easy. She'd been the one in charge for so long, and he seemed disinclined to action. Well, she had to do something.

"Yes, that might be better. You go ahead." He looked relieved.

"I'd like to serve a second meal on Saturday evening."

"Why?"

At this rate she'd be here a year and still accomplish nothing. Cassidy bristled.

"Is there something wrong with Saturday?"

"I'm not sure it's the best day."

Was he going to argue about every decision she made? Ty's face closed up. His voice dropped.

"It's just that I received a phone call from Davis. His contractor had a client drop out and so he could start on the entrance immediately."

"Uh-huh." She still didn't understand his problem.

Ty dragged a hand through his hair as if searching for patience.

"People have to come down here to eat and the only way is through the main entrance. I don't want anyone hurt."

Even Elizabeth looked frustrated.

"Surely by Friday the worst of it will be over?"

"Maybe. If it isn't, she'll have to reschedule the lunch," Ty warned.

Cassidy quashed a surge of frustration.

"I want to hold a dinner, not a lunch, and I want to get the word out beforehand," Cassidy muttered. "And once we've started serving meals, I don't think we can just stop."

"We might have to if it puts someone in danger." Ty's piercing scrutiny sliced all the way to her toes.

Cassidy knew that he would suggest she wait. He seemed to prefer a snail's pace for most things. But she couldn't just sit around doing nothing. Even if it took him a month to get everything else operational, she could still serve meals.

Elizabeth glanced from Ty to her. "We're going to have to be flexible."

Which meant *get along.*

The onus was on her. Cassidy faced Ty and chose her words with care.

"It'll take me a couple of days to get the kitchen going."

"Fine."

"Then what am I to do? I can't just sit here and wait until everything else in the Haven is operational. It would be a waste of my time, and why would you want that when we can begin reaching people right away?"

Ty's eyes blazed. The tic in his cheek gave away his irritation.

"I can't have people tracking through a construction site."

There was more to his objection and she knew it.

"We need to get people used to coming here."

"Is that what we want?" Ty tipped so his chair rested on the back two legs, crossed his arms over his chest and donned a meditative look that gave little away. A psychologist would have learned about that on day one.

Cassidy wished Elizabeth had sent her somewhere else, someplace where the director was not so afraid someone might actually accomplish something. But she also sensed there was an undercurrent to his obfuscation, so she exhaled her frustration and tried diplomacy.

"I have to think in terms of what I can accomplish in the

six months I'm here." She listed some of her ideas. "Any objections?"

"I'm sure those are all fine." Elizabeth looked relieved.

Ty didn't like her taking charge. She knew that because his chair plunked down on all fours.

"But?" She longed to shake him out of his stupor. *Just say it!*

"I'm trying to visualize how it would work."

"I cook, they eat. You said there'd been negative reaction from a gang. Maybe if they saw what this place is about, it would encourage the community."

"Exactly!" Elizabeth beamed. "I knew that's why God led you here, Cassidy."

God? Cassidy wanted to laugh. As if He cared what happened to her now. She showed Elizabeth her list of to-dos.

"A meal is fine." Ty's disinterested tone evaporated. Suddenly he was all business. "Just so long as you don't expect me to get involved down here." He glanced at Elizabeth, saw her frown and rushed to rephrase. "I mean certainly, if you need help or want some direction, I'm available."

"Right." That would be the day that Cassidy would need his direction in a kitchen.

"The majority of my time must be focused on getting the Haven ready to go."

"Of course." Let him assess. As long as he didn't do it down here. "Once I see how Thursday goes, I'll be better prepared for Saturday night. I want posters up immediately so the word gets out."

Ty could dawdle till spring but Cassidy intended to give the Haven her best shot as a repayment to Elizabeth. Then she'd move on to her dream.

"Cassidy, I knew you'd take this challenge and make it your own." Elizabeth's smile sent a dart of pleasure to her heart. "Now, let's talk about your budget."

Ty didn't even glance her way. They tossed figures around for an hour before allocating a sum specifically for groceries. Cassidy knew she'd have to be very creative to feed the number she was counting on with such a small budget. But to give Ty his due, it was hard to know how the Haven would be accepted. A little shoe leather would help her find those answers.

"I want to thank you both for what you've accomplished here today. Whatever we do is for the Lord and I know He will be pleased." Elizabeth rose, hugged Cassidy. "We're going to let you get on with your work, dear. Ty and I need to talk about some other matters. You will let me know if you need anything, won't you?"

"Thank you, Elizabeth. I hope things will work out here as you want."

"Of course they will, child. God doesn't give us dreams to crush them. You know that better than most." Elizabeth's face glowed. "I'm so fortunate I can be a part of this. I think Gail will be very proud."

Ty's handsome face wore a scowl, but only for a moment. "I have some figures in my office." He nodded at Cassidy. "We'll see you later."

Which was supposed to put her in her place, no doubt. He guided their benefactor from the room. Cassidy waited until he reached the door.

"Ty?"

He turned, lifted one eyebrow. "Yes?"

"I'm going to need at least one helper. Should I ask around, or do you have someone in mind?"

"As soon as I'm finished with Elizabeth I'll make some calls. Okay?"

Cassidy pressed her lips together, nodded and Ty left.

Still playing the part of the boss. That was fine, for now.

But if he didn't come up with someone quickly, she'd do it on her own.

Because nothing was going to stop Cassidy from doing her duty the very best she could. Then she'd walk out of here and prove to her father and anyone else who cared to watch that she was worth loving.

Ty clapped his hands over his ears, struggling to ignore the pounding as he spoke on the phone. The answer he received was not conducive to soothing the headache that throbbed behind his eyes.

For a moment he wondered how much louder it could get, then realized that the pounding came from his office door.

"Come in," he called, praying nobody would ask him to make a decision. Friday afternoon at four wasn't his peak performance time. "Hey, Mac. How are— What's wrong?"

"It's Cassidy." Mac stood in the doorway, his face beet red as he gasped for breath, shifting impatiently from one foot to the other.

"Is the kitchen on fire? What's wrong?" Ty strode toward the door, ready to investigate.

"Not the kitchen. Bring your car keys and your coat. You're going to need them." Mac was thumping down the steps before Ty could ask any more questions.

"Car keys." He shuffled through the papers littering his desk, found them, grabbed his coat, locked his office door and followed. By the time he'd closed the front door Mac was already moving around the corner of the building.

Ty jogged down the stairs and to his parking spot where the older man clung to the car door, half bent over as he puffed for air.

"What is going on?"

"Get in. I'll explain on the way," Mac ordered.

Ty steered down the snowy street, twisting and turning through a labyrinth of streets, following Mac's directions. On his own, he knew he'd never remember how to get back.

"What are we doing here? What's going on?"

"Cassidy's recruiting," Mac told him, scanning the run-down housing and less-than-well-groomed streets.

"She's what?"

"Recruiting. Inviting people to dinner tomorrow night."

"Cassidy's out here by herself?" Ty gulped, whispered a prayer for help.

"She grew up around here, thinks she knows the place well enough to handle herself." Mac glanced at him sideways. "I don't think she's aware of how tough it's become."

"Cassidy grew up around here?" Ty blinked, shocked by the knowledge. "I didn't know that."

He hadn't wanted to know anything about Elizabeth's protégée, if the truth were told. He'd heard more than enough from Elizabeth, who couldn't stop bragging about how lucky they were to get the great Cassidy Preston at the Haven. Even Jack constantly sang her praises.

"Some of Jack's new friends told him what she was doing. He told me to bring you, just in case. Then he followed her. That's the street. Go right."

Furious that she'd dragged his nephew into this, Ty cranked hard on the wheel and followed Mac's directions.

"Where?" He slowed down, took a second glance into garbage-strewn alleys and dilapidated tenement buildings. Cassidy was nowhere to be seen.

"It didn't take me that long to get you. She's got to be around somewhere." Mac's face turned a sickly gray-white. "That gang— Do you think— I mean, you hear such awful stuff—"

Ty didn't know what to think. Nothing had prepared him for this.

"They're just kids—punks with big mouths." He hoped. "Should I stop here?"

"Not yet. Keep driving. Slowly."

"Why would she do this? I told her I'd get someone to put up posters."

Three days ago he'd told her that. Today was Friday. And he still hadn't done it. She was probably fed up with his promises.

Ty gulped.

If anything happened—

"Stop!"

Ty jammed on the brakes. Mac was out of the door and down the narrow alley a second later, motioning for Ty to follow.

"Why couldn't she just cook?"

That wasn't fair and he knew it. Ty eased into a parking spot, shut off the motor and got out. He locked the doors, then wondered if it would do any good.

Realizing Mac had disappeared, Ty hurried after him. Just his luck the old guy would get bumped on the head and he'd have two of them to care for. Approaching the corner, he heard voices—loud, angry.

Ty stepped up his pace and ran smack into Mac's solid back. He shifted to move around him, but the old man clamped iron fingers on his shoulder.

"Wait."

Cassidy, wearing a thick parka and a red hat, leaned against the stoop of the oldest building on the block, listening as someone raged at her because the place was a dump and somebody ought to do something. The shrill voice soon rang a bell. He tilted upward to get a better look and almost groaned.

Red. He'd have known the raging teen and her band of unhappy chums anywhere. He caught his breath. Jack stood beside Red, eyes wide as he listened to her diatribe. If

Cassidy had led his nephew into trouble with those juvenile delinquents—

The moment Cassidy got a break, she began speaking. She didn't make excuses for Red's tough lot in life, didn't apologize for getting a chance herself and taking it, didn't even try to calm her down.

What Cassidy did do was get her message across.

"I'm really sorry, Red. If you want, we can talk about this some more tomorrow night at the Haven. I'm making a great big dinner and everyone's welcome. If you want to come, you're welcome. Bring a friend, your mom. There will be lots to eat."

"How much?" Red snarled.

"It's free. All I'm here to do is tell you so you can spread the word. I've spent a lot of time baking chocolate cakes and I'd hate to have to throw them out if nobody shows up."

"As if." The sneer was the same one Red had used on Ty the day Jack had introduced her as his newest friend.

Cassidy rose, took a step down. "Now I have to get a move on."

"What's the rush?" Red's second-in-command, a bullish boy a few years older than her, swaggered in front and shoved his pimply face into Cassidy's. "Don't you like it around here?"

Cassidy glanced over at Jack, but she didn't take the bait. Instead she scanned the crowd, her face thoughtful.

"There's only—what? Fifty people here?" She shook her head. "That won't work. I ordered meat for three times that many. If that food isn't eaten, they're going to tell me there's no point to me cooking it and the kitchen will close." She looked Red straight in the eye.

The sullen girl held her gaze for a moment, nodded once.

"You think you can stretch it to two hundred if me and the guys let everybody know? There's some old folks three blocks over could use a good meal."

"Two hundred?" Cassidy pretended to consider. "Potatoes, gravy—everything?"

"Even the chocolate cake."

"I guess I could make some more. You don't think two hundred is too many?" The challenge was obvious.

"Now you can't do it?" Red scoffed.

"Not if I have to stand here arguing with you," Cassidy shot back. "So you'll spread the word and I'll have the food ready. Deal?" She held out her hand.

The group stood to one side of the stoop, waiting for Red's reaction. Ty knew that whatever the girl said, they'd do. She had a way of commanding power. One glance at Jack told him his nephew was under her spell, too. He shuddered at the thought of where that could lead.

Red tried to stare the chef down, without success. Maybe she'd met her match in Cassidy Preston.

An audible sigh rippled through the crowd when Red grasped Cassidy's hand.

"Deal." Red dropped it a second later, turned and gave orders to her group, who began fanning out among the streets.

Ty exhaled. So far, so good.

"Hey, cook!" Red turned back. "What you gonna do if we get more than two hundred?"

Cassidy kept her cool as she faced the challenge. Ty wanted to cheer when she pulled a list from her pocket and studied it for several seconds before looking at Red.

"I'm going to improvise. Don't worry, you won't go hungry."

The crowd hooted with laughter and Red sauntered away. For a moment Ty thought Jack might follow her but Cassidy prevented that by introducing him to the remainder of the group.

"And that man over there is his uncle, Ty. He's going to be running the Haven. And that's Mac."

"Aw, you don't have to introduce us to Mac," one man called. "He's one of us."

"Okay then." She worked her way through the crowd issuing the same invitation over and over. "See you tomorrow for dinner."

By the time she reached them Ty could only gaze at her in admiration, wondering where she got her nerve. Then reality sank in.

"You and I need to have a discussion, Jack. Right after I talk to Cassidy. My car's this way." He stepped forward, then glanced around. "Mac?"

"I'll see you later, Ty." Mac waved him off.

Ty nodded, led Cassidy away from the group.

"Will you please let go of me?" she hissed and, when he didn't release her fast enough, she jerked her arm free. "This isn't exactly Beirut. I don't need a bodyguard. What's wrong with you, anyway?"

*So* the wrong question.

"Exactly what I'd like to know." Ty forced his jaw to relax. "What are you doing here—alone?"

"Inviting people for dinner. Something you didn't manage to get around to."

Guilty as charged. His temper simmered.

"I'm sorry. I got buried in work and forgot. But you could have reminded me. You didn't have to come here yourself."

She looked at him as if he was crazy. "Why not?"

"Because it's not safe. This place is a—" He glanced around, searched for the right word.

"Slum?" She nodded. "Kind of why we're here, isn't it? That's why I'm telling them what we have to offer."

Ty had to walk faster to keep up to her, which only elevated his frustration. Along with his raging headache.

"Look, I can't be responsible—"

"No one asked you to be." Cassidy stopped, glared at him. "I'm here to cook, but I'm not going to have it all go to waste because you 'forgot' to let our clients know. And I don't need you to check up on me."

"I didn't."

"Then?" She blinked, silvery-gray eyes brimming with confusion.

"Mac came racing in, said Jack told him to come get me." He glanced at his silent nephew. "Jack has the sense to know you shouldn't be out here on your own. I think he was scared. With good reason," he added to push the point home.

"Oh." Cassidy frowned at the boy. "I'm sorry, Jack. I didn't mean to scare you."

"I wasn't scared," he said, indignation rippling through his squeaky voice as he glared at Ty. "It's just that Red is a little—"

"Out of control," Ty finished for him.

"No! But she gets mad because she can't make things better," he explained earnestly.

"I think we all do," Cassidy told him quietly. She patted his shoulder, glanced at Ty. Then her eyes opened very wide.

"What's wrong now?" he demanded, wondering if he'd ever get accustomed to her chameleon personality—one minute blazing at him, the next sweetly comforting his nephew.

"Can I ask you a question?"

That soft voice, the way her fingers curled around his forearm—when two minutes ago she'd jerked from his grasp as if he had rabies. Ty couldn't figure out what was wrong with her.

"A question?" If only his head would stop hammering. "Go ahead."

"When you got here your car had tires, right?"

Ty whirled around. His beautiful baby sat on the pavement

like a wounded bird stripped of its wings. He groaned, pressed his fingertips to his temples and counted to ten.

"I'll take that as a yes." She looped one arm through his, the other through Jack's and drew them both along the street beside her as if she was in charge and they were two naughty boys who'd done something wrong. "Back to the Haven, guys. And next time when you come looking for me, Ty, don't bring your car."

Six months, she'd said?

Ty had doubts he'd make it through six more days.

# *Chapter Four*

Cassidy scooped out the last morsel of mashed potato and plopped it onto a plate. She added meat, vegetables, a roll and gravy before handing it to Ty.

"You're timing is excellent. We're down to mostly aroma and three rolls." A surge of triumph rolled through her weary body.

"How many?" he asked, scanning the room.

"Two hundred and ninety-five plates not including the seconds we served."

He studied her face for a moment before grabbing another plate and dividing his meal. He handed the second plate to her.

"It's time for you to take a break," he insisted when she tried to set it down. "You've been going at it for hours. Now enjoy your success and relax."

Cassidy wanted to argue, but she was too tired. Besides, Ty had come through with a dozen volunteers who were busy scrubbing the pots and pans. Everything was under control.

"Come on," he coaxed with a lazy grin. "You know you wa-a-ant it."

"What does that mean?" she asked, trailing behind him to an empty table.

Ty did a second take then laughed.

"I keep forgetting you haven't been in the country for a while. It's something the kids say. Jack uses it on me all the time."

"Speaking of Jack—where is he?" She glanced around the room curiously.

Ty scanned the area, then scowled.

"Supposed to be clearing tables. Which clearly isn't happening."

So everything was not well between the two. Cassidy wasn't surprised given the arguments she'd overheard the past few days.

"Maybe he's taking a break, too." She sampled the beef and judged it perfect. "Teens don't usually stick at anything as boring as cleaning without supervision."

Ty's fork hit his plate so loudly that Cassidy thought the tired crockery would shatter.

"Look, I can't watch him all the time. I've got things to do."

She waited till he looked at her.

"I wasn't criticizing. I know you've been running on all cylinders."

He grimaced. "Sorry. Again."

"Forget it. You're tired, I'm tired. Comes with the territory."

"You don't look tired. You look like you've just been granted your dearest wish."

She felt the heat flood her cheeks and shrugged.

"What can I say? I love cooking."

"And you're very good at it, though I imagine I'm not the first to tell you that." He sampled the beef then tilted his head in Davis's direction. "He certainly has a gift for conversation."

Cassidy chewed her roll thoughtfully.

"Davis could make a friend out of his worst enemy. He's as lovable as a teddy bear." She told Ty of the many times her friends had helped her through a rough afternoon though she never mentioned why it had been rough. Some things didn't need sharing.

"Were you ever—" Ty paused, raised an eyebrow. "Romantically involved?"

"With Davis?" Cassidy made a face. "No way."

"Why not? Is there something wrong with him?"

"Do not get me started on Davis's faults." She scrambled to escape this conversation. Judging by the way Ty was studying her it wouldn't be easy. "Besides, I don't get romantically involved."

"Why is that?"

Cassidy pushed her plate away, her hunger dissipating like this morning's fog.

"Let's just say I'm not good at putting my faith in people." *Especially men.* She rose. "I'm going to get a cup of coffee. Do you want some?"

"No, thanks." Ty grimaced, shook his head. "My stomach couldn't take it. Water is fine."

"I'll see if there's any cake left, too." She hurried away without a backward glance, anxious to regroup before he cornered her again. As she headed for the counter, someone grabbed her arm.

Cassidy whirled, her nerves automatically zipping to alert as she reacted by assuming a defensive stance.

"Hey!" Her assailant held up both hands. "Just me. What's up, cook?"

"Red." Cassidy unclenched her fingers and smiled at the abrasive gang leader. "Don't do that again, okay?" She exhaled slowly. "Did you enjoy your dinner?"

"Yeah, it was cool. You gonna do this every night?"

"Maybe. I'm not sure exactly how it's going to work yet. Ty and I need to work it out." She turned the tables. "Would you come if I did?"

"Nah." The lean redhead slouched against a table, watching as Cassidy poured two drinks. "But my mom might. If I can keep her sober long enough."

Been there. Done that. Cassidy felt a twinge of regret for the young girl's future.

"You let me know if I can help."

"Yeah. I'm sure."

"I mean it, Red. If there's anything I can do, I'd like to help." Cassidy met her stare without flinching. "That's why the Haven is here. To help."

Red broke eye contact, focused on her chained boots. "She needs a job."

Cassidy didn't hesitate.

"Has she ever worked in a kitchen before?"

"At home, every day," the girl quipped. "Why?"

"I might be looking for some kitchen help. Part-time only, till after lunch. Could you get her to come in and see me?" Experience had taught Cassidy that mornings were the worst time for drinkers. Having a reason to get up sometimes helped.

"I don't know." Red's suspicion was evident. "You're serious?"

"Very."

The teen studied her for a moment before she nodded. "I'll see what I can do."

"Good." Cassidy picked up her drinks and headed back toward Ty. "See you later."

"Hey, cook."

She paused, glanced over one shoulder at Red.

"That cake was awesome. If I was into cooking, that'd be my fave."

"You don't cook?" The redhead shook a negative response. "Ever?" Cassidy asked in disbelief.

Red shrugged. "I don't starve but I'm not into slaving over a stove. I can get by on pizza."

"You want to taste real pizza, you come to the karaoke night we're planning," Cassidy challenged. "If my pizza doesn't make you want to learn to cook, I'll give you ten bucks."

"Deal. Easiest ten I'll ever make." Red sauntered away with a cocky sway.

Cassidy froze for a moment as the glimmer of an idea stewed in her brain. Then she snapped out of her fog and hurried back to the table where Ty sat frowning.

"What did she want?"

"Who? Red?" Cassidy set down the cups then took her seat. "I offered her mother a job."

"What?" His jaw jutted forward.

"It's only for a couple of hours every morning."

"But I had already chosen someone."

She pinned him with a glare born from frustration. "I can use two people or you can give the other person something else to do."

"Because?"

"Because there's a reason I want Red's mom."

"What reason?" His tone oozed skepticism.

Cassidy tamped down her frustration by chewing on a raw carrot. Did he really not get it?

"If her mother is working here, doesn't it seem unlikely that Red will cause problems for us?"

Ty had the grace to look embarrassed.

"Sooner or later I'm going to realize you're always two steps ahead of me and stop putting my foot in my mouth." He surveyed the room with a frown. "I still don't see Jack."

"I wasn't exactly watching, but I don't think he's been around since before Red and her group came in."

"That kid is going to be the death of me."

"Don't be silly. Jack's a great kid. You don't have to worry about him. He's probably sitting outside, shooting the breeze with the other kids."

Ty grimaced. "I hope not."

"Why? Are you some kind of snob?"

"Me?" He wrinkled his nose. "No."

"Then why shouldn't Jack make friends?"

"Friends?" Ty snorted. "I'm not against him making friends. It's the vandalism, assault and theft I don't want him to learn."

"All the kids in this neighborhood are into those things?" Cassidy knew she'd struck home when a look of chagrin washed over his face.

"I wasn't saying that and you know it. But a lot of the gang members are Jack's age. Can you blame me for wanting him to avoid them?"

No, she couldn't. But she'd come from this area and she hadn't fallen in with any drug lords.

"It's a tough area, Ty. The kids here don't have a lot to do with their spare time. You can't blame them. Sometimes it's easier to join a gang and be part of something than it is to always fight the problems at home alone."

"Is that how it was for you?" he asked softly.

"Sort of," she admitted, knowing he'd immediately assume she'd been like Red. "My mother died when I was quite young. I was the oldest with two younger sisters. But my dad was hardly ever home so I had to play mom, which didn't leave a lot of time to hang with anyone."

"It must have been a painful time for you." His voice dropped, softened. "I'm sorry, Cassidy. I need to watch what I blurt out."

"No, you don't. But you need to stop making assumptions. You can find good and bad people everywhere, Ty."

"Believe me, I do know that. I didn't stay in Ir—the military very long before that lesson was driven home." He dragged a hand through his hair. "It's just that Gail left Jack in *my* care. I don't want to mess up."

"Who says you're going to?" Cassidy jerked her head toward the group of preschoolers playing in one corner. "You didn't mess that up. Your day-care center is a real hit."

"It's not mine," he protested. "Not really. The women had the idea. I just helped them pull it together. But so far the co-op idea seems to be working."

Everything about Ty changed as he watched the children. His face lost that ragged, careworn appearance; his eyes softened to a robin's-egg blue. His chin dropped and his shoulders relaxed their rigid structure. He'd be a pushover as a daddy, which made her wonder why Ty and Jack didn't jibe.

"I suppose you didn't have anything to do with the seniors' lunch I'm apparently cooking next week, either?" Cassidy chuckled at his surprise. "You can't keep secrets around the Haven."

"I wasn't intending to keep it a secret, really. I simply hadn't gotten around to speaking to you about doing it. Will it be too much?" Ty's earnest face echoed his tone. "I wouldn't dare ask except they came to me with the idea."

"I think it's wonderful."

Many of her neighbors, people who'd helped her out in those dark days of her youth, now needed her help. It felt good to give back. "It's not a big deal to make some soup and sandwiches, cut up some fruit."

Ty studied her as if he didn't quite understand. Well, why would he? Sometimes Cassidy didn't understand herself. She'd thought six months here would be nothing short of a penal sentence. Instead she was finding a freedom and joy she hadn't experienced in years.

Ty must be experiencing something of the same for he'd finally stopped assessing and started doing.

"Thank you," was all he said.

"You're welcome."

As they ate, the room slowly cleared out. A few people stopped by to say thank you and offer to help clean up, but most scurried away as if they couldn't believe their luck in getting a free meal. The groceries Davis had collected from the church and left in bags near the door disappeared quickly causing Cassidy to wonder how long it had been since some of the older ones, the helpless ones, had eaten.

"You never did tell me what Red said to you."

"Hmm?" She glanced at Ty as the idea came flickering back. "It wasn't so much what she said. Well, it was, but—"

"You don't have to tell me." His eyes narrowed. "But you got an odd look on your face and I wondered if she'd said something bad."

"Not bad. She gave me an idea. But I have to let it percolate for a while. Then I'll tell you about it."

Ty grinned. "By then it will be too late for me to stop whatever you're thinking of doing."

"Exactly." She crossed her arms over her chest and smiled smugly.

He rose, hooting with laughter as he carried his plate to the rack by the kitchen. Cassidy followed, slightly amazed that this was the same man she'd debated with such a short time ago. Ty actually seemed glad she was planning things.

"So, when's the next big meal?"

She blinked, startled by the question, then grabbed opportunity and told him her plan. He listened, nodded.

"If you can handle it, I'm fine with your decision. Do you want to keep the same helpers?"

They discussed staffing for a few minutes. Then Jack reappeared and Ty's demeanor altered.

"I'd better go see what he's been up to."

"Ty?" Cassidy touched his arm while her brain told her to mind her own business.

"Yes?" he asked, a hint of impatience evident in the glance at her hand.

"I probably shouldn't say this but don't push him too hard about the gang, okay? He's new here, he's trying to fit in and he's almost a teenager. If you jump too soon he won't let you in on what's on his mind and believe me, you want your nephew to confide in you."

He frowned. "And you know this because?"

She grinned.

"I told you, I had two younger sisters. I learned about teens while being one. I'm sure I've forever damaged their psyche or something because of our battles." She held his gaze. "Just listen before you do anything else."

Ty considered then slowly nodded. "I'll try."

It was more than she'd expected.

While her volunteers finished cleaning the kitchen, Cassidy sat down to work on her menus. She'd been at it for an hour when she realized the others had left and she was alone, save for the thin woman standing in the doorway.

"Can I help you?"

"I am Irina Markovich. My daughter tells me you have job for me."

"You must be Red's mother. Come in. Would you like a cup of coffee?"

As soon as Irina moved into the light, Cassidy caught a glimpse of bruising above Irina's left eye and noted the slightly stiff movement as the woman sat down. Her heart sunk as she recognized the signs. Irina had been beaten.

Briefly Cassidy laid out her needs and the duties the job would entail.

"Is this something you might be interested in?"

"I would very much like to help you in k—in the kitchen."

In fact the expression on Irina's face hinted that the job might be the answer to a prayer. As if God actually answered prayers.

Cassidy scolded herself. It wasn't the Almighty's ability she doubted, it was her prayers He didn't seem to heed.

"Good. Can you start Monday morning?"

"Yes."

"Then you're hired." Belatedly Cassidy remembered Ty. "If you don't have to rush away, I'd like you to meet the director of the Haven. Mr. St. John gets final say, but I don't think he'll have a problem with you."

"I will work very hard," Irina assured her.

"I know you will." As they walked up the stairs to Ty's office Cassidy searched for common ground. "Your accent— it's Russian, isn't it?"

"Yes." Irina's pale cheeks glowed bright red. "I try—I am trying," she corrected, "very hard to speak good English."

"You're doing very well," Cassidy assured her. Then she started singing in Russian. "I worked with a Russian chef who insisted I learn his language."

Irina's self-consciousness disappeared as she responded with a Russian joke. They were both laughing as they walked toward Ty's door, which was probably why Cassidy didn't hear the argument until it was too late to turn away.

"It's not safe to be wandering the streets after dark, Jack. I've told you how rough—"

Cassidy rapped on the door and opened it quickly, before they were forced to overhear any more.

"Sorry to interrupt," she apologized. "I wanted you and Irina to meet." She introduced them. "And Jack, of course." She smiled at the boy, flinching at the rebellious glint in his eye. "Irina's going to start helping me in the kitchen on Monday morning."

"Welcome. I hope you'll enjoy it here, Irina." Ty shook her hand but didn't get to say anything else because Jack interrupted.

"Are you Red's mother?"

"Yes, I am." Poor Irina cringed as if embarrassed by her daughter's activities.

"Well, we don't want to keep you, Ty," Cassidy said pointedly. "I just thought you'd like to meet. Irina and I have some stuff to talk about."

Cassidy turned and headed for the door but just before she stepped through, Ty grasped Irina's arm.

"Wait!"

A whimper whispered past the woman's white pinched lips as she drew her arm away and tucked it against her side.

"I'm so sorry. I didn't mean to grab so hard." Ty looked at Cassidy helplessly.

"I fell down this morning. My arm hurts." Irina stared at the floor.

"I'm always injuring myself," Cassidy said. "My friends used to say I'm like a walking bandage. What was it you wanted, Ty?"

"I wanted to ask Mrs. Markovich something." Ty paused a moment, his forehead pleated. "One of the construction workers mentioned the name Markovich earlier today in reference to basketball. Would that happen to be your husband?"

Irina's face tightened. She nodded once.

"Perhaps he'd be interested in helping coach a children's team," Ty said.

"I do not think he has much time." Irina moved toward the door. "Excuse me, it is later than I realize. I must go."

"I'll see you Monday," Cassidy called as the other woman hurried down the stairs and outside, quickly disappearing into the street.

"She acts like she's afraid of something." Jack stood behind her, watching.

"Maybe she is." Cassidy turned, smiled at him. "Thanks for pitching in today, buddy. You did a great job and I appreciate it."

"Thanks!" Jack glanced at his uncle reproachfully.

"I'm tired. I think I'll get my coat and go home." Cassidy almost made it to the bottom of the stairs before Ty's voice stopped her.

"Jack wants to finish a chess game with Mac. Why don't I drive you?"

She didn't need time to consider it.

"Thanks. I'd appreciate it. I'm so tired my legs barely function. Too much time off before I came here, I guess."

"Meet you at the front door?"

"Thanks." Cassidy returned downstairs to check everything, clicked off the lights and grabbed her purse and coat. She waited for him on the stoop outside, watching the neighborhood fall into its night patterns.

"You look a thousand miles away."

Ty held out a hand and despite her misgivings, Cassidy took it and let him escort her down the icy stairs, then let go.

"Never left Chicago." She walked beside him toward his car, noting the shiny new rims and wheels.

Ty must have tracked her gaze.

"Don't even ask," he ordered, his mouth tipped in a grim line.

"Okay."

"Isn't it a beautiful evening?" He rested a hand on her arm as they walked over the partially frozen yard. "When I was a kid, my dad took Gail and me outside after dark every Sunday night so we could watch the stars come out. We never felt the cold. We'd lie on the snow and peer up into the sky until each of us had identified at least two constellations and seen a shooting star. Then we'd go in for hot chocolate, giggling and laughing long after we were tucked up in bed."

"Sounds like you had a good childhood."

"Yes." He held the car door, waited for her to get inside. "I think that's what I'd like most for Jack to remember about his youth. Happy times."

"He will."

"I hope so."

Cassidy directed him to the little home Elizabeth had provided, and when they arrived, invited him in for tea.

"I don't have much of a yard, but you're welcome to flop down on the snow out back if you want."

"Thanks anyway. Maybe another time." He grinned. "Say, five months from now."

"Chicken."

"Absolutely." Ty followed her inside, paused to study the cherished pieces she'd brought back from Europe. "Should I light the fire?"

"Would you mind? Starting that fire usually takes me an hour. Then it's time to put it out and go to bed." She hung their coats up, then moved to the kitchen to brew tea.

Last night she'd made a pie for her elderly neighbor, but since he'd left for a winter holiday this morning it still sat on her counter. Cassidy cut two slices, then carried everything to the living room.

"Have a seat," she said, wondering what Ty was thinking about as he peered so intently into the flames. He'd relaxed a little, lost the fan of lines around his eyes.

He chose the overstuffed armchair that sat in front of the window and sniffed where her herb pots sat.

"I can smell mint, parsley and dill but those are the only ones I'm familiar with. Guess I wouldn't make it as a foodie."

"You named most of them." She added a sprig of the spearmint to his tea. "Everything tastes better with fresh herbs."

"Having sampled your wonderful cooking, I agree." He

accepted the chunky mug, sampled the contents. "Mmm, delicious. I've never tasted anything like it before."

"It's a blend I make for myself," she explained. "Since I've come back, I find the food either too sweet or too salty. I've taken to drinking a lot of tea. It cleanses the palate and—"

One glance at his face told her she was rambling. She handed him the pie.

"Sorry. I hope you don't find that too sour."

He judged it perfect.

"If sweet and sour are the only differences you've noticed since you returned, you're lucky."

The way he said it pricked her curiosity.

"You must have noticed some differences when you came back, too."

"I did."

"Like?" Oh, that was stupid. His sister had just died. Of course he'd notice a difference.

Ty tensed. His fingers pinched whiter around the mug. His back straightened. He waited several moments before answering.

"The smells. People's attitudes. Sounds."

"Is that why you aren't able to sleep much?" She was getting personal but Cassidy needed to understand why he startled every time there was a loud noise, why he fussed so much about Jack if his nephew wasn't in school or easily spotted nearby.

"What makes you think I don't sleep much?" He smiled when she reminded him that he'd beaten her to work this morning. "You're right. I don't. Too much nervous energy, I guess."

He hadn't looked energetic at all, but Cassidy had little time to dwell on his words as Ty quickly turned the conversation.

"Why do you want Irina Markovich in the kitchen?"

"Red mentioned she needed a job. I need the help." She shrugged. "We'll see how it goes."

"I'm pretty sure she's been beaten," he told her.

"You think Red did it?"

"No." His blue eyes sought hers, held them until she broke the stare.

"Red told me her mother drank."

"Uh-huh. Did you see Irina's reaction when I touched her arm?" He leaned back but kept watching her. "There's something else going on there, Cassidy. Watch yourself."

"Red and Irina aren't going to hurt me," she scoffed.

"I didn't say *they* would." Ty sipped his tea and watched her, his gaze mesmeric. "You think you know this neighborhood because you used to live here, but it isn't the same place as it was. Things change. People change."

"I'm not naive. I take precautions. I've had to." *Don't talk about the past.* "Some of the places I've lived weren't great. But I won't live in fear just because there are bad people around. I've already wasted enough time living like that." She clamped her lips closed, refusing to expose any more of her battered soul.

"I'm sorry," he apologized. "I'm not trying to run your life. I'm just—worried."

"That surprises me," she admitted, flicking her fingers over the handmade afghan her last boss had given her. "I never took you for the worrying type."

Ty's eyebrows lifted. "What type did you take me for?"

"You're always talking about God to Jack." Cassidy shrugged. "I didn't think Christians were supposed to worry."

"Touché." The corners of his lips lifted, but he was not amused.

"So?" She waited for an explanation.

"I guess I worry more since Gail died."

Cassidy knew that wasn't all of it, but she also sensed that Ty needed to say more. So she sat quietly and waited.

"It's not that I don't trust God to handle things, I do. It's just that—her death was so unexpected. I felt like I lost control of things. Like the world was spinning wildly around me and I couldn't find anything to grab on to. I still feel like that sometimes. I guess my faith isn't as strong as it should be."

"Well, you don't have to worry about me. I've been taking care of myself for quite a while." *Without his or God's help.*

Ty studied her, a funny look washing over his features.

"And you don't want me messing up your system?"

"I think you've got enough on your plate with Jack and the Haven." She leaned forward. "He's a good kid, Ty, but if you feel your world's spinning, he must certainly feel the same, don't you think?"

"Of course. But I don't want his grounding to come courtesy of Red and her gang."

"You said your sister spent a lot of time here. Did Jack ever come with her and help out?" She waited for his nod. "Then I'm sure he met some unsavory types, but he seems to be a very centered kid. I don't think Red or anyone else will persuade him to do something he doesn't want to. I think he's just trying to find his way in his new world."

"Maybe." Ty stared into the flames, his face highlighted by their dancing glow. "He doesn't talk much, you know. I was hoping that time would ease his grief, that we could talk about her. But with everything so wild at the Haven, there's hardly a moment."

"Then make one." Her heart ached for him. "The Haven will be around next year and the year after, but Jack won't and he's your primary responsibility. He needs to know you're there, that you love him and care about him. That you want what's best for him."

Cassidy suddenly realized that she was advising a psychologist on family matters.

"Sorry," she apologized, embarrassed by her outburst. "I'm sure you know exactly how to treat your nephew. I should mind my own business."

He didn't contradict that, but a cute little grin fluttered across his mouth. "Like that's going to happen."

She lifted one eyebrow. "Touché."

They spent some time discussing the programs for the coming month. Ty shared some ideas he'd been pursuing, stunning her with the scope of his plans.

"Wow. These are big ideas. Are you sure—"

"Rest assured I haven't been pursuing dead ends," he snapped, setting his cup down hard on the coffee table. "I want things well under way before the spring."

"What happens in the spring?" Ty seemed suddenly intense and Cassidy didn't understand why; a few days ago she'd had to push him to allow a single meal to be served.

"Sooner or later we'll have a grand opening. Before that happens I want to make sure the Haven is doing everything my sister intended it should."

"I see." Cassidy opened her mouth to ask another question, saw his glance fall on the picture she'd hung above the settee.

"What's that?" he asked, rising to take a better look.

"A drawing." She did not want to talk about *her* dream.

"A very detailed one. Of what?" He studied the sturdy columns, the wide front porch, the lush urns that guarded the entry.

"A friend drew it for me. Would you like more tea?"

Questions hovered in his scrutiny but Ty didn't ask them. He simply watched her for several moments before checking his watch.

"I'd better go. Jack's probably won by now."

"Does he always win at chess?"

"Usually. He's a strategist. Thanks for the pie."

"I wrapped up the rest of it for you to take home. I know teenage boys get hungry and I won't eat it. I'm on a diet."

"I can't imagine why. But thank you." Ty pulled on his jacket, accepted the pie from her. Still, he didn't leave.

The stretching silence unnerved her. Cassidy couldn't look at him.

"You did a great job with the meal," Ty said, his voice soft. "The turnout was far better than I expected and everyone enjoyed your cooking. Including me."

"It was fun," she admitted. "I'm going to ask Davis if his church will sponsor the grocery night every Saturday. That stuff disappeared in seconds."

"There is a food bank a few blocks over."

"Which none of those people will use and we both know that." She waited, wondering why he hesitated.

"You could ask him tomorrow. Jack and I are going to his church. We could give you a ride."

Cassidy shook her head. "No. Thanks. I don't do church."

"Okay." He shuffled from one foot to the other, shadowed eyes watchful. "Well, at least you can sleep in a little later tomorrow morning. Good night."

"Good night." She closed the door behind him, drew in a deep breath to modulate her racing heart. Without saying a word, Tyson St. John could make her feel like she was sixteen and about to get her first kiss.

She glanced at the rendering on the wall, felt the squeeze of determination grip her insides.

But he couldn't get her to talk about her dream. Not until she was ready.

Not until there was no possibility that he or anyone else could ruin it.

# Chapter Five

By eleven on Monday morning Cassidy and Irina had almost finished preparations for the first seniors' lunch at the Haven.

"The sandwiches are ready. Now we can focus on supper."

"You will continue to serve evening meals?"

"Six nights a week is my goal."

"But you have no day off. It is pushing too hard."

"I take Sundays off. Soup and sandwiches with a doughnut for tonight won't kill me, Irina. Besides, after Saturday's success, I want to keep up the momentum."

"I am game." Irina grinned.

"Good. Now watch carefully because the doughnuts will brown very quickly. Flip them over once. As soon as they're finished, scoop them out and let them drain. But don't spatter yourself and don't rush. Okay?"

"Yes." Irina nodded.

A quick learner, Irina was soon frying doughnuts as if she were in a production line. Almost finished, she yelped as hot oil spattered her hand.

"Let the water cool it," Cassidy advised, turning the tap on.

The injury was slight, but she fished out the last two dough-nuts herself.

"I wasted a lot of time for you." Irina patted her hand dry.

"No. Anyway, your being okay is more important. We'll glaze them in a few minutes, and then all we have left are veg-etables to chop for tonight's soup." She saw the other woman waver and knew Irina stood upright only through force of will. "Let's take a break."

"But the luncheon?"

"Is ready. Come on. Relax for a minute."

Cassidy set some of the sandwiches on a plate and poured coffee, but it wasn't until they were seated and Irina held the bread to her lips that Cassidy noticed her shaking hand. Irina caught her stare and quickly thrust her free hand under her thigh, keeping her eyes downcast.

"What's wrong, Irina? You're shaking."

"I will get stronger," she reassured, as if afraid she'd be fired.

"You're doing fine. But I don't think you're worried about work. It's something else. Couldn't you tell me? I'd like to help."

Irina said nothing for a long time, but a tear crept out from under her lowered lid, then another until she was openly weeping. Feeling helpless, but guessing the woman needed this physical release, Cassidy waited.

"I'm sorry." Irina dabbed her eyes. "I will get back to work now."

They went through the same routine every morning for the next two weeks, and every time, Cassidy encouraged, hoped, waited. When nothing happened, she finally sought out Ty for advice.

"You can't make people get help, Cassidy. It usually takes something big to make most people act." He accepted the coffee she'd brought, his blue eyes soft with sympathy. "It must be doubly hard for Irina."

"Why? Most days when she arrives, it's clear she's in pain. But I don't think she's had a drink since she started." Cassidy couldn't comprehend an otherwise strong woman's refusal to free herself and her children from such a situation.

Secretly Cassidy constantly compared Irina with her mother, recalled the many nights in bed listening to the arguments between her parents and often, the sounds of violence. Yet the next morning, her mom had always acted as if everything was fine.

"It's as if Irina's waiting for things to get better."

"No doubt she is." He dragged a hand through his freshly trimmed hair, leaned back in his chair, his gaze pensive. One finger tapped the desktop. "I'm sure she came to this country full of hopes. Her husband probably did, too. But things haven't worked out the way either of them wanted."

"So he terrorizes his family?" Cassidy knew too much about this part. "Maybe somebody should take a couple of rounds out of him."

"Like you?" Ty teased. One glance at her face and his chair dropped to all fours. His cup hit his desk, spraying coffee droplets over his arm. His face tightened. "Don't even think about it, Cassidy."

"I don't have a death wish. But Irina's wound so tight, I'm afraid she'll crack. She needs to talk to somebody." An idea flickered to life. "Could you?"

Ty's face blanched and the self-assured man vanished. His fingers stopped tapping, pressed tight against the desk surface. His eyes darkened to navy.

Cassidy felt his fear as if it were a tangible object in the room. "Me?"

"That is what you do—talk to people. Counsel them. Isn't it?"

"I did. Once." Tiny lines fanned out around his pinched lips. "But—"

"Just a conversation."

"I don't think I could—"

"Please, Ty? Irina's hurting and she needs someone to talk to. Isn't that why the Haven is here? To help?"

Cassidy watched him wage some internal battle. Finally he inclined his head, once.

"All right. But I won't push and I won't tell you what we discuss."

"Of course not." She was offended that he thought he had to say it. "When?"

"I'll ask her to fill out some papers tomorrow morning."

"Great."

From his grim countenance, Ty didn't think so. Maybe it had something to do with the argument she'd overheard last night between him and Jack.

"Is everything all right, Ty?"

He'd been shuffling through some papers but his hands stilled at her words, his head lifted. "Why do you ask?"

"No reason." She pretended to peer out the window. "I didn't see Jack around yesterday."

"He and Red had 'things to do.'" Exasperation was clear in his tone.

"She's not a bad girl, you know." She ignored his laugh. "I think she'll come around when she starts seeing changes happen in the community."

"From your lips to God's ear."

He was brooding. Cassidy couldn't stand there doing nothing. "Get up."

"Huh?" He glared at her. "I can't go anywhere. I've got tons to do."

"Don't we all? Get up." She tapped her foot on the floor, waiting for him to rise. "Lose the tie, Ty."

"Hah." His fingers went to the perfect knot, fingered it while he studied her in that scholarly but perplexed way that said he was trying to figure her out.

"Undo it. Come on, counselor. Dinner's almost ready but I've got coleslaw to make so get rid of that tie."

"What is this about?" He loosened the tie, drew it off and laid it on his desk.

"Winter doldrums, I think. Let's go." He didn't move quickly enough so Cassidy looped her arm through his and drew him along with her toward the gym. She opened the door, flicked on the lights and pushed him inside.

"You cannot have this room for a kitchen," he said, but a faint light now glowed in the indigo irises.

"You've been taking funny lessons from Davis." She grabbed a basketball, dribbled it to the back of the gym and took a shot. "That's one for me."

"One what?"

"Point. Loser owes the winner a favor. Best out of ten." She set up, then netted the ball perfectly. "Two for me. Get ready to pay up, director."

In an instant the ball was lifted from her fingers. He tossed a rim shot, rested his hands on his hips in a cocky stance and waited for the ball to sink.

"You should have told me the rules first, chef. Don't you know cheaters never win?"

Never one to give up without a fight, Cassidy dug in her heels and hung on for the toughest game of one-on-one she'd ever played. And lost.

"So let me get this straight. I won. Therefore you owe me a favor. Wasn't that how you described this game?" Ty's smirk ruined the attempted solemn look.

"Arrogance is not one of your better features. Have I mentioned that?"

Truthfully Cassidy couldn't find a thing wrong with his features. His flushed face shone with pleasure, his mouth quirked up in that mocking grin he often used and his body stance was assured, confident—nothing like he'd looked earlier.

Her arm still tingled where he'd pushed it away while reaching for the ball. She got caught up staring into his eyes. Her breathing suspended.

For once no inner voice warned her about trust.

"What's going on?" Jack stood in the doorway.

The moment shattered.

"Cassidy was teaching me about basketball."

"She's teaching you?" Jack slid the ball from his uncle's hands, dribbled it while he frowned at Cassidy. "Did you mention you went to college on a basketball scholarship?"

"I may have forgotten to mention that." Ty held his palms up. "She didn't really give me time to explain."

"Conned by a pro." Cassidy shook her head, winked at Jack. "Disgusting."

"Worse than that." Jack's gaze seemed fixed on Ty's beaming face. "He usually cheats."

"I don't need to cheat." Ty's chest puffed out. "I'm too good."

"Yeah?" Cassidy lifted the ball from Jack's hands and zinged it at Ty. "Prove it, hotshot. Jack and I against you."

"That's not— Hey!" he yelled as Jack stole the ball, raced across the floor and made a basket.

The next half hour passed in laughter and good-natured jeering, but at the end of it, Ty remained the point leader.

"You do know CPR, right? Because I'll probably have a heart attack anytime now." He bent over, resting his hands on his knees as he caught his breath. He turned his head, shot her a grin. "But it was worth it just to know you owe me. You, too, Jack."

"We were playing for something?" Barely winded, Jack continued to shoot baskets with deadly accuracy.

"Favors," Cassidy huffed, clutching her side. "You and I both owe him one. I need to get back to the kitchen. Life's easier there."

"Are we having food at the karaoke on Friday night?"

"Pizzas." She dragged herself toward the door, almost wishing she'd saved her energy for work. But it had been so much fun.

"Wait up." Ty walked beside her, held open the door. "Coming, Jack?"

"Nah. Can I let some of the guys come and shoot baskets?"

Ty paused, nodded.

"Let me know when they get here. Mac can supervise."

"They're not going to rob the place." Jack's ruddy face grew belligerent. "Like there's anything to rob in this dump."

A tic flickered in Ty's jaw but he kept his voice level.

"There is a liability issue and I won't endanger your mother's work. So please tell me when they arrive. Okay?"

"Fine." Jack slammed the ball against the hoop so hard the echo rattled around the empty gym.

"Sorry to put you in the middle of that," Ty apologized, letting the door swing closed behind him.

"Don't worry about me." Cassidy had a thousand questions, all of them to do with the boy who'd been happily playing one minute and metamorphosed into a grouch the next.

"Lately I can't seem to say or do anything right with Jack. I'm very concerned about him. He's getting more and more sullen and I don't know why."

"Have you asked him?" She winced at the glower he shot her way. "I know, you're the psychologist and you know all the procedures, but I imagine it's different when it's someone close to you. So?"

He said nothing as they walked the hallway, but at the stairwell Ty paused.

"Jack doesn't talk to me."

"Why—"

"Other than the few cursory words he needs to get through the day, he very seldom says anything—unless it's to tell me how badly I'm doing something."

"I'm sorry." Her heart pinched at the lines appearing on his face. "I know you're trying, Ty. And I don't think it's you, particularly. He's almost a teenager."

He wagged his head slowly from side to side.

"It's me. Jack resents that I'm here and his mother isn't. Natural, certainly. But I'm responsible for him and I'm trying my best."

"It can't be easy, I know that. Do you mind if I try something Friday night?" She might live to regret her spur-of-the-moment decision but Cassidy couldn't stand by and see this family fracture.

"Such as?"

"Well, it's taken so long to get the karaoke night planned—not your fault," she added before he could protest. "I wonder if Jack, and some of the other kids, too, if they show up, could help me assemble the pizzas. I'll have the ingredients ready. There are lots of plastic gloves. They could have fun putting together different combinations."

"They might ruin everything." His brows drew together like thunderclouds massing. "I'm not sure it's a good idea for children to be in the kitchen."

"In the kitchen's a lot better than on the street," she shot back then wished she hadn't. "They're not going to get hurt sprinkling cheese on dough, Ty. I'll do the oven part."

"I thought you had helpers to prepare the food ahead of time."

"I do. And we will." Getting him to agree to her ideas was like pushing cement uphill. "The Haven is for everyone, right?"

He nodded slowly as if he wasn't quite sure he believed it.

"We have the seniors' lunches, we have the evening meal. We have the day care. What we don't have is something for the older kids to do. I doubt many of them will actually sing, but we could get them involved through the food. Maybe in time it would become a Friday-night thing for them to host— like a coffee house. You did say Jack was interested in the musical stuff at Davis's church," she reminded him.

"He just bought a bass guitar—without my knowledge." Ty's chagrin needed no translation. "I guess there could be worse things, but—"

"Maybe he'll start a trend and the kids will come here to rap."

He lifted one imperious eyebrow at her vernacular but Cassidy knew he was considering it because he tapped his fingers as he considered her position, finally nodding.

"Ask them. But don't be hurt when they turn you down flat."

"Oh, ye of little faith."

She was quoting Scripture now? Cassidy scooted down the stairs toward the kitchen, but paused halfway.

"You promise you'll talk to Irina tomorrow morning?"

"I said I would. Remember, you owe me a favor."

"No problem. Just let me know."

"I will, Cassidy. And you will pay up."

Funny how she trusted that Ty would exact revenge and it didn't bother her a bit. In fact, she was actually looking forward to it.


"Cassidy said you must talk to me." Irina stood in the doorway Tuesday morning, fingers knotted, eyes wide with fear. "I do—did something bad?"

"According to Cassidy you've been doing very well. Please, sit down."

He wished he'd had more time to prepare, though if the truth were known, Ty doubted he'd ever be ready to do this again. He checked his watch and realized it was very close to noon. Cassidy probably thought he'd forgotten all about his promise. As if.

"You are not well?" Irina leaned forward over the desk, her face perplexed.

"I'm fine. Just a little nervous," he admitted ruefully.

"You are nervous of me?" She blinked her surprise, the rigidity leaving her body. "I did not know I was scary."

"It's not you, it's me. I'm not very good at this job yet."

"You will get better. People like you."

He hoped she was right.

"I have some forms I need you to sign." He pulled out a file, opened it and indicated where. "It's to do with the government regulations."

Ty waited while she carefully read each line then etched her signature at the bottom. Her sleeve moved up and he saw the circle of bruises around her wrist.

When she was finished, Irina set down the pen, caught him staring.

It was now or never.

"Are you all right, Irina? Is it safe for you to go home today?" He kept his voice soft, his tone mildly questioning. "Are your children safe?"

For the first time since he'd met her, she did not look away when the subject of home was broached. This time she simply sighed, leaned back against the chair and shook her head.

"No. They are not safe. No one can be safe there."

"They can't unless you make it happen. You're the only one who can change things." So far, so good. He'd remembered all the right words.

"I do not know how."

"Maybe I can help. Tell me what it's like, Irina. I won't judge," he promised. "I won't pry. I'll only try to help."

"My husband is not a bad man."

"But he does bad things?"

She nodded slowly.

"When he gets angry?"

A few more gentle probes and she poured out the ugly situation, wept at the mess their lives had become. Ty offered a word of encouragement now and then, but he didn't press and he didn't hurry her. What she had to say had been bottled up for a long time. It would not evaporate easily or quickly.

But as he listened, an odd thing began to happen to his insides. Like a bud beginning to open, he felt the first stirrings of life nudge at the fear. His gut unclenched enough to let him take a breath and comprehend what Irina wasn't saying.

"I do not know what will happen next," she whispered.

"You know what you want to happen though, don't you?" She nodded.

"Can you tell me?"

She hiccuped a sob, dashed a tear from her cheek and nodded.

"I want to go to sleep at night and wake up in the morning feeling good. I want my children to come home and play without fearing. I do not want to worry anymore."

*Neither do I, Lord.* The cry came from his heart.

"I don't want you to worry anymore, either, Irina. So anytime you need to get away, to find a safe place, you come here. Okay?"

Irina straightened, lifted her proud head and studied him for several moments.

"Yes."

"Good. Now I want to tell you some things I know." Ty explained what experts had learned about abusers, about triggers and the escalation of violence. "I don't want you to be afraid, Irina. I want you to be smart. I want you to keep yourself and your kids safe."

"Yes." She checked her watch, rose. "I must leave now." But she didn't go. She hovered in the doorway as if other things prayed on her mind.

"Is there something else?"

"May I talk to you again?"

Ty blinked. She wanted to come back?

"Anytime," he said sincerely, a flush of success suffusing his soul.

"Cassidy says your sister wanted the Haven. I am glad of this. It is a wonderful place. I think God will bless it."

"I think so, too." He watched her leave then rose to peer out the window at the swirling snow that covered the city.

Maybe, just maybe, he wasn't totally washed up.


"Isn't it fantastic?"

Cassidy had to lean close or be drowned out by the woman wailing a country-western tune with the karaoke machine. Ty inhaled her fragrance, a light rose scent.

She looked nothing like she usually did. Gone were the figure-hiding chef's whites. Tonight Cassidy wore slim-fitting, worn jeans and a silvery-gray sweater that emphasized the quicksilver tones of her eyes. Two thin silver earrings matched the necklace the circled her throat, sparkling against the raven black of her hair. Beautiful.

"I never imagined so many kids would turn out. And they don't seem to mind the adults that are here."

He nodded, when he spotted Jack in the corner, tuning his guitar with another boy.

"Who's the guy with Jack, do you know?"

"I think his name is Boe, something like that. It's hard to hear." She grinned as if she was having the best time.

Ty's stomach somersaulted at her radiance. Cassidy was ready to take on as many challenges as life threw her way. He wondered if she thought him old.

"I noticed Irina stopped by your office." She tilted her head to one side.

"I can't tell you anything, Cassidy."

"Well, I know that! I only hoped you were able to help her."

"We'll see." He wouldn't tell her how desperately he hoped that session was the first of many he'd conduct. "How come I don't smell pizza?"

"You had dinner—" she checked her watch "—two hours ago."

"That long?" He laughed at her glower. "The thrill of cooking for this place beginning to wear off?"

She pulled him to a quiet corner, motioned to a chair.

"I expected it to get boring." Her wide-eyed beauty entranced him. "When I came here I was dreading my six months."

"You never let on. Or told me how it happens you're here." Ty wanted to know more about her, details that explained the quirky personality he'd only glimpsed.

"You're very persistent."

"Makes me a good psychologist." He ignored her sigh. "Go ahead."

"Six years ago I was about to pursue training at Le Cordon Bleu in Paris."

"Aren't there such schools here?"

"Oh, yes." Her fingers busied themselves smoothing the plastic tablecloths she and Irina had cut from red gingham. "But I wanted Paris."

"Because?"

Cassidy studied him as if deciding whether or not to trust him.

"A fantasy of mine. The first step, anyway."

Ty puzzled over the way she said it, reverently, as if she hadn't quite achieved her dream, even after six years in Europe. There were layers to this woman—deep, uncharted territory that he now realized she wouldn't share easily. And he wanted to know.

"So you were ready to leave and what? You lost your ticket?" He'd hit too close to the truth.

"You could say that." Sadness drenched her face, her eyes stormed with emotion.

"I'm sorry, Cassidy." He laid a hand on hers, squeezed. "Can you tell me?"

"No." In a turnabout, she tossed her somber attitude and flashed her glittering smile. "Anyway, I was penniless, about to be homeless and scared stiff. Elizabeth showed up, offered me a chance to realize my dream on one condition—that I'd repay her generosity sometime in the future with six months of my time. So here I am."

Some of the kids, Jack among them, hurried over now that there was a break between songs. They began hassling Cassidy. Their banter rippled while Ty studied her. Her records put her at twenty-nine. Six years ago—she'd gone to Europe when she was twenty-three. A tender age for a world traveler.

Yet in Cassidy's case, it fit. She wore maturity like it was an outlook she'd had for a long time. He remembered she'd talked about sisters, raising sisters. Had it happened then?

He wanted to learn more.

"Ty?" Two community workers, friends of Gail's, had organized the evening. He'd left them in charge, but now they wanted him to talk to the crowd.

Ty pushed away his questions about Cassidy and concentrated on explaining what the Haven was about and invited those who wanted to participate or help to sign the sheets by the door.

"If you want to hang around, we'll be enjoying fresh pizzas as soon as they're ready," he offered before turning the microphone over.

With music filling the room, the workers started board games, initiated shuffleboard and generally saw to it that everyone was involved. In the kitchen, the kids gathered around the center island as Cassidy showed them how to roll out pizza dough.

Ty leaned against a wall, admiring her easy rapport as she coaxed and cajoled each kid. Jack flourished under her tutelage and was soon chopping vegetables like a pro. But the size of the knife he was wielding worried Ty, so he pushed away from the wall, ready to intercede.

"Leave them be."

"It's dangerous, Mac."

"They're not babies. Most of them probably carry switchblades longer than that. Besides, I doubt Jack would appreciate your interference in front of his friends."

Ty frowned at him. "But—"

"Look." Mac nudged his shoulder.

Ty twisted, watched Jack lift a knife from a smaller boy's hands. The boy's face darkened with anger but before he could say anything, Jack pointed out that they had chopped up enough toppings. He handed the boy a block of cheese and a grater, dared him to shred the whole thing.

"Jack's finding his way. Don't interfere, Ty."

Ty studied the boy until he felt someone watching him. Cassidy.

She arched one eyebrow, as if to ask if he approved, and Ty nodded. She continued explaining how much of her homemade sauce to place on the dough, but she kept returning to Jack, teasing, brushing flour off his nose, hugging his shoulder. Jack glowed.

"She's good with him."

Ty nodded. *Maybe a little too good.* Envy pricked his ego as he watched their easy camaraderie. Cassidy made communicating with Jack look so simple, and yet Ty had never found anything more difficult.

Vigilance from twenty-odd pairs of eyes made sure the pizza was cooked to perfection. Under the chef's direction, the kids served everyone a steaming slice before they sampled their own. Laughter echoed through the room.

"Makes it worth all the work, don't you think?" Cassidy stood by Ty, surveying the energized room.

"I guess."

"You don't sound convinced."

His old nemesis, fear, chewed at its leash, broke free.

"I'm not."

Her face sobered as Cassidy studied him. "What's wrong now?"

"The Haven is supposed to be a place for people who can't help themselves."

"And?" Her lips crimped tight.

"I'm not convinced these kids need help. They have nothing to do but make trouble and they're using us for a good time." He watched Jack pick up his guitar, follow the instructions of an older boy. "What happens next week when we can't amuse them? Or feed them?"

The silver in her eyes melted to liquid mercury. She grabbed his arm, drew him out of the room and into the hall.

"Is this really about feeding some kids, having a little fun, Ty? Or are you upset about something else?" Cassidy sounded irritated, but underneath her frustration, a deeper emotion was clear. "Maybe you've never spun your wheels in a neighborhood where there doesn't seem to be any way out. Maybe you can't understand why a little space and time with others is so important to a kid who feels totally alone and out of control in his world."

"I'm sure—"

"Let me finish." She pinned him with her gaze and this time the anger snapped and crackled throughout her entire body. "If it's the money you're worried about, Ty, I'll pay for the pizza ingredients. If it's the evening of free time you've lost, I'll stand in for you one night."

"It's not the time or the food costs." He felt like a curmudgeon, but the fear that gripped him would not be silenced.

"Then I don't understand your complaint. But I'll tell you one thing. Before you begrudge those kids a few moments of fun, check their expressions. Look. They found a moment of happiness here, Ty. For a little crack in time, they can be kids—can joke, laugh and forget about doing or saying the wrong thing. They don't have to be afraid."

She leaned in and the curve of her silky black hair brushed his cheek.

"Look at Irina's kids."

Ty looked. While Red scoffed at the unmusical sound Jack's guitar was making, Irina's other two children sat, smiling and laughing.

"You want to make a difference in this community? You have to start with its future—its children."

When she finally faced him, Ty recognized that the emotion she'd hid was pain. Longing. He wanted to ask about it, but she didn't give him a chance.

"Everybody wants the best for their children, Ty. If they can find a place they'll trust with their kids, this community will throw open its door to you. But better than that, they'll get behind you, back you so strongly you won't need the city or anyone else to police it. They'll do it themselves, because the Haven will feel like it's theirs."

He'd never imagined Cassidy felt so deeply about this place.

"You want the Haven to fulfill Gail's dream." Her voice grew so soft he had to lean in to hear it. "And it will. But sometimes you have to stand back and let it grow without trying to prune. Have some faith, Ty. They're not all bad kids."

A buzzer sounded. Cassidy hurried away to rescue another pizza.

Ty remained in place, watching. Thinking.

He wished he could be like her, see only the best in people. But he knew better. He'd watched Donnie retreat further and further from their family, saw the friends who'd dragged him into a counterculture where violence and drugs sapped away his little brother until no one could save him.

Ty had lost too much not to fear.

He couldn't afford to lose any more.

Tomorrow he'd begin formulating a new set of rules for the Haven. It was the only way he knew to combat the worry and fear that filled him.

*What about God?* a voice inside his heart asked.

God? Where was God when those soldiers— He slammed the door shut.

It wouldn't be as bad if they had some rules. A few. To keep things safe.

He hoped.

## Chapter Six

Cassidy almost groaned at the series of neon-orange signs littering the hallway walls Monday morning. Twenty-five new rules.

"Good morning."

It *had* been.

"Morning."

"I see you've noticed our rules."

"Hard not to." She sidestepped Ty, hustled downstairs to get the coffee on. She needed a large cup—extra strong—before she opened her mouth again.

"I thought perhaps you wouldn't bother coming in today."

Cassidy twisted her head to frown at him.

"Why would you think that?"

"Well, with the storm and everything. I'm not sure the delivery trucks will be able to get through the drifts." The blue cashmere sweater did good things for his eyes.

"Uh-huh." Cassidy concentrated on measuring the grounds, poured in the water and inhaled deeply as the first fragrant drops filtered through.

Ty lounged in the doorway as if waiting for congratulations. But she refused to utter one word until coffee had percolated through her brain and taken off the edge.

"Did you have a good day off yesterday?"

"Fine." Visiting with her sister's two hyper kids always drained her. But Cassidy loved their lack of inhibitions, envied the freedom they enjoyed. What she hadn't enjoyed was her sister's news about their father.

"Is something wrong?"

"Why?" She kept her back to him, poured a dollop of cream in her mug, tapped the side of the coffeepot as if that would hurry it. *Don't say a word.*

"Because you're doing it again."

"Again?" She did turn then, scowled at him. "Doing what?"

"Fiddling. Fidgeting. Trying your best not to look at me."

"Oh." Unable to wait a moment longer, Cassidy slid her cup under the dripping spout while she poured from the half-full carafe and filled her cup. With the carafe back in place she took a swig of the fresh brew and closed her eyes, waiting for it to rein in her temper.

Her determination to stifle her criticism cracked. She set the cup down as gently as possible, then turned to face him.

"What's wrong with you?"

"Nothing." Ty frowned, glancing down at his clothes as if they were the problem.

But then maybe they were. Maybe his need for control was an attempt to keep himself clean, to make sure nothing negative or distasteful touched his antiseptic world.

After a moment he seemed to realize he'd missed the point.

"I think I'm going to need one of those, too." He poured himself a cup, walked to a stool and perched on the top. Once seated he studied her with a pensive glance.

"You look like you want to hit me. Unclench your fingers and tell me what I've done wrong now."

"What are those hideous signs?"

"Ground rules for the Haven."

"No running." Cassidy shook her head. "What is this, kindergarten?"

"With all the snow, the floors get wet and with that tile—" He held his palms up. "It gets slippery."

"No pets?" She slapped her hands on her hips and squeezed, trying to temper her anger. "Are you telling me someone actually brought an animal inside this shelter?"

"Not yet but—"

"Lights out at eleven o'clock?"

His face actually brightened. "That's for when we get the beds open. So that everyone will know what time— What?"

"If we finally get someone in the door, I doubt they'll stay after reading your rules."

"We have to have some rules, Cassidy. You must recognize that."

"Of course. But do we have to plaster them all over the walls? This place is supposed to welcome people and when I walked in and got smacked in the face with all those 'do nots' I nearly turned around and left." She took another drink. "And I work here!"

"You never approve of anything I do." He picked up his cup and headed for the door, hurt by her disapproval.

"Not true. I understand that everyone has to abide by a set of regulations or we'll have chaos. But can't we put the rules for sleeping here in the area where they belong? And could we forget some of the others until needs arise?"

His face stiffened; anger glinted from the blue irises.

"It's too bad Elizabeth didn't hire you to run this place. You seem to know exactly how it should be done."

Cassidy wished she'd stayed home.

"I'm sorry. I shouldn't have said anything."

"When you first came here I had the impression you could hardly wait to get out. Now suddenly you're involving yourself in all aspects of the Haven."

*Which were none of her business.*

Cassidy got the point, but she couldn't let it go.

"This place, the people who come here—they're not simply people to feed." She struggled to clarify for herself as much as for him. "When I first came here they were all nameless, faceless people, but now there's Mac and Irina and Red and Jack." *You.*

"And you want to do your best for them."

"I want to do more than that. When a homeless woman or man sits down at the table, I want them to experience a meal they won't forget. I want them to enjoy it, to relax, to find—"

"Hope?"

Cassidy nodded, surprised he'd tapped into her dream so well.

"It's like this is my restaurant and I don't want anyone having a bad experience here."

"You don't think they'll have that experience if the signs are up."

"I think anyone who reads all those rules will be so preoccupied with not breaking them their experience here will be ruined."

She held her breath, waiting for his anger.

"I didn't realize you were so passionate about this place."

"I didn't, either, until I realized I could be feeding my sisters, my nieces, anyone who needs a hand up."

"Working with you is always one step forward, two steps back." Ty dragged a hand through his hair, his face rueful.

"Not exactly a compliment." She wrinkled her nose.

Ty huffed a laugh. He rinsed out his cup and set it in the wash-up area before facing her.

"There's no way around having some rules, Cassidy. But I'll try to make my signs a little less off-putting." He thrust out his hand. "Friends?"

"Yes." She shook it, knowing how much it cost him to backtrack. But Cassidy didn't have time to dwell on that because the heat of his fingers against her skin left her breathless. It took every ounce of willpower to back away from his touch.

"No free time for me this morning." Ty sighed.

"Now might not be the best time to ask this, but since I've already stepped on your toes, can you tell me what you have planned for Jack's birthday?"

Ty gulped like a guppy searching for air.

"Birthday?" He glanced at his watch, closed his eyes. "I completely forgot."

"The only reason I'm asking is because I heard some of the gang members talking and—" She hesitated, but Ty had to know. "It sounded like they might be planning something."

"Something?" He tilted one eyebrow.

"They clammed up when they realized I was listening."

"I see."

Cassidy knew he was thinking about his rules. Fear followed Ty around like a child, constantly tugging at him. She didn't understand why, but figured that, like her, he probably had something in his past that caused it.

"Let me help, please, Ty. If we put our heads together we can surely come up with something a kid Jack's age would like. And maybe we can cut the gang off before they do something regrettable."

"I don't—"

"Good morning." Irina's arrival cut off all conversation.

After greeting her and agreeing that he had time to meet with her in the afternoon, Ty left the kitchen.

"He is such a kind man," Irina said as she peeled potatoes. "I have done many things wrong, but Ty never laughs at me. He just keeps teaching me how to understand my husband."

"I'm glad you're getting help, Irina."

"Ty helps me understand. Listen."

As Irina repeated what she'd learned in her sessions, Cassidy applied the information to the situation she'd endured with her father.

She found few answers.

"For so long I did not understand how my husband could hurt me and then become loving and kind." Irina's face brimmed with sadness. "That is why I let it continue. I kept hoping he would go back to being the man I'd married. I know now that will not happen."

Cassidy wanted to encourage the woman to talk, but she didn't want to pry so she worked silently, listening.

But her bitterness wouldn't melt.

"Ty says it's very hard when the abuser is usually so kind and gentle. For a little while everything seems fine, but it isn't. We are all waiting for the explosion."

Cassidy flashed back to her home when she was six and she wanted a bicycle. They didn't have enough money for a new one, but one day her father had come home with a damaged one that he repaired. Only with the vantage point of time did she realize how patient he'd been with her, how careful with his restoration.

She'd enjoyed the bright red bike for two glorious days before he'd flown into a rage and smashed it beyond repair for something she'd done wrong. Could that be why she preferred not to attach herself to anything—because someone might take it?

"Ty says I am not helping when I try to smooth things over. He says that I—hmm, what is the word?—enable my husband." Irina used the knife to emphasize her words. "Like I am saying it is okay for him to be violent and mean. It is *not* okay."

"No, it isn't." Cassidy couldn't recall how her mother had handled her father's temper.

Some things were best forgotten.

"I have thought a lot about what Ty says. It helps me understand many things. But I still have one question."

Cassidy had a hundred. First on the list, how could a man hurt the very ones who loved him most? Who trusted him to keep them safe?

"I want to know why he does it. What caused my husband to become this—monster?"

*When you find out, let me know.*

"I hope Ty can help you."

"He will." Irina paused for a moment, her face serious, eyes pensive. "He is a sad man, is he not? Ty, I mean."

"Sad?"

"He carries it with him like a shawl—no, I mean a shroud. Sometimes I feel so badly for always bothering him when I know he has many problems of his own."

"Ty is here because he wants to help," Cassidy said, amazed by Irina's accurate description of their director. "That's why he came."

Irina's soft smile intrigued her.

"He calls me at home sometimes."

"Really?" Cassidy struggled to hide her surprise.

"He pretends it is to ask me a question about one of the children." Irina's voice dropped. "He is checking to make sure I am not hurt. Ty does not think I should stay in my home."

"Where are you supposed to go?" For a man who hadn't wanted to talk to Irina, Ty was certainly getting involved in her life.

"Ty says that if I and the children stay in our home, my husband must not. That he must get help before someone gets hurt. But I do not think I can leave." The last part came out on a whisper. Then Irina said no more.

Later that afternoon Cassidy saw her return to the Haven, swathed in a wool shawl, covered in white flakes. Her counseling session must be very important if Irina was willing to walk to the Haven through so much snow.

Cassidy was putting the finishing touches on the evening meal when Ty walked into the kitchen.

"I'm opening up beds for tonight." He smiled at her start of surprise. "While you've been busy cooking these past weeks, I've been organizing your friends' donations. Davis and company should be here in twenty minutes to help me set up the rooms."

"Great." So he and Davis were in contact. Cassidy wondered if they'd discussed her, told herself not to be silly. They'd probably talked about football or some other sports subject men shared in the depths of winter.

"Could we get some cereal and milk to serve in the morning? You don't have to come in. I'll be here all night anyway so I can slip down and get things ready."

"I can do it. No problem." She studied him. "You certainly work fast."

"What can I say? You're my inspiration. I couldn't sit around watching."

She blushed. "What about Jack? Where will he stay tonight?"

"Here. There's a small room off my office that I've prepared for him."

"Oh." Cassidy could imagine the boy's irritation at not sleeping in his own bed. "Are you going to supervise every night?"

"No. Elizabeth's setting up a rotation of people."

"Irina's been telling me some of what you two talk about. You certainly have a knack for asking the right questions. She's thinking about what you said."

"Good." Ty didn't seem encouraged by her words. He leaned against a support post and gnawed on his bottom lip, his gaze fixed on some distant point.

"Something wrong?"

"I don't know."

Concerned by his pallor, Cassidy poured two mugs of hot chocolate from the carafes she'd made for the evening and beckoned him to pull up a stool at her worktop.

"What's wrong?"

"It's not wrong—exactly. It's—unexpected."

Cassidy passed him a plate of cookies, waited.

"Irina's been talking to some of her neighbors."

"She's a big fan of yours." Cassidy frowned when Ty squeezed his fingers into fists and pressed them against his thighs.

"She's sent them to see me." His voice dropped to a murmur. "To talk to me."

"That's nice."

"No, it isn't. I can't talk to them, Cassidy." He hunched over the table, hands cupped around the mug as if he was seeking protection.

"But you're a psychologist. Talking is what you do, Ty." Her gentle reminder seemed to infuriate him.

"Was. It *was* what I did." He tossed her a stormy glare.

Cassidy wrapped one hand over his and discovered it was shaking. Shock made her hang on, thread her fingers into his. Ty looked so—helpless.

Before she could ask for an explanation, a loud crack from the street outside shattered the silence. Ty's head jerked right, toward the sound. He bolted upright, knocking over the mug of chocolate. As the brown stain pooled across the table his eyes glazed. He sucked in soft huffs of air in rapid succession, as if he'd been running, yet his chest didn't move. His hand squeezed around hers, crushing it.

"Ty?"

He didn't respond. Cassidy tugged on her hand, but he would not release it.

"Let go, Ty." She yanked hard, unable to quash her own fear, though she knew he would never deliberately hurt her. "Ty!"

He came back slowly, his blue eyes a bemused slurry of confusion.

"Yes?"

"What's wrong with you?"

"I'm fine. Did I do that?" He used the chocolate mess as an excuse to avoid her scrutiny, grabbing a cloth and mopping it up with a slowness that irritated.

"You're not fine. I want—"

"Hey, cookies. Can I have one?" Jack dropped his backpack on the counter and stretched out a gangly arm to snare three. "Any more of that—to drink?" He glanced from the smeared brown mess to Ty.

"Sure, but you'll probably spoil your dinner." Cassidy poured another cup, set it in front of him.

"Thanks." Jack's grin teased her. "When have you ever known me not to eat dinner?"

"Good point." Though she loved listening to Jack's after-school banter, Cassidy couldn't shelve her concern about Ty.

"Jack, we're going to be staying here tonight." He'd finally finished his cleaning. "You won't need anything from the house, will you?"

Jack's face turned from beaming to bitter.

"You said I could have Boe over tonight."

"He could come here. Only him though. Till nine. Try to

keep it down, will you? I don't want the place noisy when I'm trying to get people settled."

"Settled?" Jack frowned. "What people?"

"It's supposed to get very cold tonight. I thought this would be a good time to make the Haven live up to its name." Ty cocked his head toward the booming voice from upstairs. "That's Davis. Want to help us make beds?"

"No."

"Suit yourself. See you later." Ty left.

Jack glared after him a minute before turning to Cassidy. "Would you have time to read over my English assignment?"

"I'd love to, Jack. If there's time after dinner. I have to get breakfast ready, too."

Jack surged to his feet, eyes seething with temper.

"Never mind. I don't want to be a bother to anyone."

"It's not like that, Jack, and you know it. This is my job. I have responsibilities."

"Yeah. So does he." He jerked his head upward. "Worthy jobs that I should understand, right? Fine. I'll call Boe and we'll amuse ourselves. Maybe Red can come, too."

"Ty said just Boe," she reminded.

Jack rolled his eyes.

"He's got a lot of people counting on him. Keeping this place running, trying to raise you—it can't be easy."

"I know. Ty's busy. So are you. Helping the needy. Great. Don't worry, I won't bug either of you." He rose, sauntered to the door.

"Jack?"

"Yeah?" He scowled at her.

Cassidy pointed to the dirty dishes, watched as he carted them to the sink and dropped them on the washboard.

"Happy?"

"No. You're old enough to understand that you can't always

come first." She debated whether to say it and then decided a dose of reality couldn't hurt. "I don't like it when you act like a baby."

"Well that's how he treats me, like a stupid little kid who can't blow his nose without help." The last word erupted on a tide of emotion.

Though Jack wheeled away, Cassidy caught the sheen of hurt.

"I know it's hard, honey." She laid a hand on his shoulder, but he jerked away from her touch. "It won't always be rushed like this."

"Won't it?" His glare oozed disbelief.

"Ty's not avoiding you. Once he gets everything running smoothly you'll have lots of time to do things together." Cassidy stopped because Jack didn't believe her, and, if the truth were told, she wasn't sure she believed herself. Ty and Jack didn't seem to connect on any level and she couldn't figure out why. "Don't be too impatient. Give it time."

"Yeah. Sure. Sorry I took it out on you." He offered her an apologetic smile.

"You can talk to me, Jack. Anytime. About anything."

"Thanks." But he didn't hang around. "See you."

"Later," she promised. "With your lit homework."

As Jack clumped up the stairs Cassidy realized that the neediest people at the Haven weren't only those who used its facilities. It was time to get Ty and Jack doing something together. In her pocket, her cell phone jiggled against her leg.

"Hey, sis. How goes it?"

"Cassidy, you might want to sit down."

"Why?"

"I just had a call from Dad. He wants to see us."

A black tide of rage rushed across Cassidy's brain, drowning out everything but a policeman's voice from the past.

*"Your thief was your father, Miss Preston."*

## Chapter Seven

*K*eep asking questions.

Good advice, Ty told himself.

He glanced at the expectant faces of the family crowding his office on Friday afternoon and wondered why God had sent them. God knew his desperate yearning to be free of this mental paralysis that trapped him in a world where he relived the same horror over and over again.

"So what do you think?" the belligerent teen demanded.

"You tell me." Tension stretched across the room the way static air portends a storm. "Your father is working two jobs to pay the rent. Your mom is taking every shift she can to put food on the table. Your two sisters are waiting tables to pay for their clothes. What's your contribution?"

Ty listened to the kid's outburst, then posed new questions to get the boy to see he didn't require the wardrobe advertised by a basketball superstar. Finally the boy offered to take on some of the chores at home. The family left amid good-natured teasing.

Ty sagged with relief and glanced upward.

"Thank You, Father," he whispered with heartfelt appreciation.

Outside his office, renovations proceeded in starts and fits. He thought he was immune to the noise until something shook the building and he was catapulted back to his nightmare. It took every ounce of remaining strength to push through the shroud of anxiety. Just like now.

Once alone, Ty scanned the room searching for escape. He grabbed the box holding his telescope and his coat. He was almost at the stairs when Cassidy caught him.

"How'd it go?"

"Fine." He shifted the case, scrambling for a way to make his escape.

"I knew you could help them. You're good at—that stuff." She grinned at him as if he'd just won the lottery.

"Refereeing, you mean?"

"Yeah, that." She chuckled at his feigned annoyance. "Or in your language, counseling. You have a knack for asking the right questions."

"Thank you."

"You're welcome." No guile lingered in the silver depths of her gaze, no hidden meaning or pretended emotion. Cassidy seemed an open book.

Ty wondered why it was that whenever she was around him, the veil of the past dissipated and he became energized, connected to the present, whole. She only had to start talking and suddenly he began believing he could push past the immobilizing grip that swamped him and do something really worthwhile.

Was it because she was so wholly involved in the present that she had no time for the past?

"Where are you off to now?" she asked.

"The roof." Ty knew she'd been up there a couple of times with Jack.

"You go up there a lot. Why is that?"

He shrugged. "It's quiet. I don't hear the building noise and I can think."

"Oh. Nice day for it. After such a miserable January we deserve some decent weather. I noticed you added a couple of benches."

"I thought we could use it as a kind of retreat. But I don't want clients up there." The words spilled out without thought; he couldn't stop them. "It's too dangerous."

"The roof is totally enclosed." Her forehead furrowed in confusion. "Isn't it?"

How to explain this constant nagging dread?

"It's not for use by anyone but you and me. That's a rule, Cassidy."

"Another rule?"

Ty held her gaze until she shrugged.

"Fine." She didn't blink, didn't look away.

Ty itched to get away, to fight his personal war alone. But a faint shadow lingered at the back of Cassidy's eyes. She wanted something.

"Do you need me?"

She didn't answer immediately. Her brow lowered as if debating some internal issue. Finally she shook her head.

"No. Nothing urgent. The details for Jack's party are in place. I talked to Boe. He's spoken to some of the others. They'll show up after dinner tonight. Okay?"

"Thank you." The tic of warning twitched at Ty's jawline. "I wish Jack had some friends other than gang members."

"You make it sound like Boe's all about chains and tattoos. He's not that bad."

"Really?" He glanced out the stairwell window. "The cops were here today. There's been some vandalism in the area. Again."

"That's hardly new."

"Exactly what I mean."

Cassidy's smile died.

"Have any of them done something to make you believe they're behind this latest incident?" Silver sparks flared in those expressive eyes. Her lovely mouth slanted down. "Do you have even a morsel of proof that any one of those kids Jack hangs around with is involved in vandalism?"

"No, but you only have to listen to that girl."

"Red?"

"Who else?" He made a face. "She's a poster child for problems."

"She's trying to change things the only way she knows how. You'd better not say anything against her to Jack," Cassidy warned. "He's infatuated with her."

"Give me some credit." Ty shifted the case to his other arm, impatient to forget about his failure as a stand-in father. "Thanks for your help with the party. I'd intended to do more, but—"

"Those people needed to talk to you. It's no big deal."

She said the words she thought he wanted to hear, but she wasn't finished. Ty waited, knowing Cassidy would say whatever was on her mind. She'd never been shy about that.

"I'm sure you're squeezed for time, but I wish you could do something with Jack. He wants to be part of things here."

"Isn't he helping you out a couple of afternoons a week?" It had been one of his stipulations in allowing his nephew to jam with his "band."

"With me. Yes. What he really wants is to be doing something with you."

Ty couldn't suppress his sharp burst of laughter.

"Right."

"It's true. He's lonely. He feels left out. You and I are always busy but Jack stands on the sidelines, watching us and feeling useless."

"I've suggested plenty of ways he could help."

"Help you?"

He pretended to think about it. "Well, no."

"That's what Jack wants. The Haven was his mother's idea. He wants to help you make it succeed, but he can't do that if you don't include him."

"Cassidy, he's mad at me all the time. He hates it when I talk to his friends. He breaks the curfew I gave him. Exactly what would you like me to include him in?"

"Something. Anything." She met his glare with her own.

Ty closed his eyes, raked a hand through his hair and sighed.

"I'll try and come up with something we can do together. Okay?"

"Yes." She grinned. "It *could* be fun."

"Yeah. Fun." With a rebellious almost-teen who thought his uncle was a basket case. Oh, yes, fun was tops on the list. "Anything else?"

Cassidy cast a speculative glance at his telescope case.

"Irina asked me to remind you about her friend coming, in about an hour."

The groan almost escaped him. But Ty choked it back. He set his watch's timer, thanked her and ascended the stairs to the peace of the roof.

Ty closed his eyes and inhaled the cool air, letting it wash his soul clean. Then he got to work setting the telescope into position. Though cloudy now, the sky was supposed to clear off before evening. Perfect conditions to check out the constellations.

Ty considered asking Jack to join him, but tossed the idea. The kid already thought he was a very uncool nerd. No way would he be interested in seeing Mars or a new nebula Ty thought he'd found.

Finally satisfied that everything was ready, Ty pulled the cover into place.

When night fell in Chicago, morning would be breaking half a world away. The sky would flash with fire as explosions dotted the landscape. If he closed his eyes, if he relaxed even for a moment and opened his mind he would be back in an instant, seeing…

His watch's alarm shook Ty free of the blackness. He returned to his office to listen to another problem. But in its deepest recesses, his soul begged for healing, for a chance to be free of the fear that he was not in control.

Cassidy studied Jack's face as he caught his first glimpse of the guitar-shaped cake she'd baked and decorated. She began singing "Happy Birthday." The kids remained mute. Thankfully, Ty's smooth tenor quickly joined in.

"It's awesome." Jack couldn't quite smother his grin. "Thanks, Cassidy."

"You're welcome. You'd better blow out all those candles before they light the place up."

He did, missed one and blushed in the shamed embarrassment of youth, daring a sideways glance at Red before quickly looking away.

Cassidy set down a stack of plates at his elbow.

"Cut away," she said with a smile.

"Is it the same cake you made before?" Red eyed the big knife Jack wielded.

"A little different. More fudgey. You let me know what you think."

While Jack passed around slices of his birthday cake, Cassidy poured two mugs of coffee and handed one to Ty, relishing the shared moment.

"Thanks." He sipped. "Who's the giant with the red cap?"

"Walter Something. He's Jack's latest friend." She smiled her thanks when Red set two pieces of cake before them. "Why?"

"Just wondered if he's going to cause problems."

"Why would you think that?"

"Someone used a pick on the fire door in the gym last night." He studied each face as if searching for the culprit.

"It happens." She didn't want anything spoiling Jack's birthday. "You can't stop everything. We do the best we can. If something goes wrong, we pick up the pieces."

"I do not need to pick up any more pieces, thank you."

Cassidy knew him well enough to interpret the darkness in his glare as anger.

"Your sister didn't die because you didn't stop it." What could she say to help him?

"My brother did."

He'd talked about Donnie before. Cassidy hoped he would tell her more.

"I told you he ran away from home?"

She nodded.

"He got in with the wrong crowd, started using drugs. Eventually he was living on the streets, even under an abandoned cement bridge." He rubbed the bridge of his nose as if to ease his stress. "On Donnie's birthday, at Christmas, Easter, Gail would ask around till she found him. She'd make sure he was all right, buy him a meal, give him warm clothes, that kind of thing. She'd beg him to come back, but he never would."

"He died around here?"

Ty nodded.

"New Year's Eve. Gail had taken him some gifts from us. He hawked them all for drug money, all but a sweater I sent. Donnie loved the color blue and that sweater was a vivid electric-blue. Somebody wanted it, there was fight and he was stabbed."

"Oh, I'm sorry, Ty." Her heart ached for the misery flickering through his eyes. "But it wasn't your fault. You couldn't have known."

"Maybe not then. I was just a kid. But I know more now. Jack is the spitting image of Donnie. I take precautions with Jack because I *won't* lose him, too."

His rules. That's why. Cassidy's heart ached for him. She wanted to tell him that rules couldn't stop tragedy, that it happened in spite of the best-laid plans. But Jack's birthday wasn't the time to get into it.

"Things happen, Ty. Nobody can stop all of them." She pasted a smile on her face thinking of how she'd prayed for a happy family and God's nonresponse. "Come on. Jack's finished his cake. Let's give him his gifts."

"Yeah. Sorry." His lopsided smile tugged at her heart.

"Sometimes it's good to talk about the past. It helps let it go." *Liar.* No amount of talking would ever free Cassidy from her own ugly past.

Shopping wasn't her forte but Jack seemed to appreciate her gift card from a skateboarding shop.

"Thanks." Jack hugged her quickly, cheeks reddening at the whistles and catcalls.

"You're welcome, sweetie." She caught Ty watching them.

Jack enthused over the small trinkets the other kids gave him, laughing freely at their jokes about his music as he unwrapped extra strings for his guitar, a pick, CDs. But it was Ty's gift that rendered him speechless.

"It was your uncle Donnie's. He never used it much. I thought perhaps you'd enjoy it."

Jack carefully lifted the small remote-controlled airplane from the box. He trailed a fingertip over the wingspan, touched the bright red cockpit. He looked at Ty, hopeful.

"Will you teach me to fly it?"

"Sure." Ty glanced at her, grinned.

Her heart gave a bump of joy for his happiness.

"Cool." The other kids crowded around to admire the plane. Jack joined in but every so often his gaze slid to his uncle as if he was seeing him in a new light.

Cassidy wanted to cheer. At last, something they could do together. Maybe flying that plane would forge firmer bonds between them.

For once Cassidy wished she believed in prayer.

For the past two weeks, Ty had told himself that if he just got through today, this hour, he could have an hour on the roof with the stars. But for the past two weeks, he'd managed only half an hour of pure solitude peering through his telescope.

He was overstressed and he knew it.

The flashbacks happened more frequently now, spinning him out of the present and into the chaos he'd try to leave behind. He seldom slept more than a couple of hours at a time and he couldn't focus. That's why he was constantly on edge, waiting for another disaster.

Cassidy had no such problem. She glowed. Ty caught himself waiting for a chance moment to talk to her, to watch her, to bask in her joy.

She started a community cooking class, which quickly blossomed into three to accommodate women working different shifts. The kitchen hummed with activity from early morning to late at night. Her students sang her praises loudly and clearly.

Which was great, but the more they came, the more they sought Ty's help on parenting, or job difficulties or something else he felt utterly incompetent to answer. So he did what he'd been trained to do and kept asking questions until his clients discovered the answers they needed.

At least God had answered that prayer. So far his clients

seemed satisfied and no one seemed to notice that he struggled through, losing his focus, mistaking names, sweating.

But his prayer for healing had not been answered.

He had to get his post-traumatic stress disorder under control or risk impacting his ability to help. That's why he was down in the kitchen—to corner Cassidy, to get her to head people off before his entire calendar filled up with people looking to him for help.

He'd been here twice—both times she'd been on the phone, adamantly refusing to meet someone. Though curious, Ty didn't pry, and besides, if she asked for his help, he wouldn't have any answers to give.

"Cassidy? Are you here?" he called.

The kitchen seemed unusually silent for four in the afternoon. Two pots gently bubbled on the stove, a huge bowl of Mac's favorite bread pudding cooled on a sideboard while the oven wafted a robust tomato aroma that set his stomach growling.

Apparently she was out.

Ty turned to leave, heard the steel door in the stairwell creak open.

"Come on, lean on me. It's not far now."

Ice chilled his veins as two figures entered.

Jack, his face bloodied and his clothes torn, hung on to Cassidy, his breathing harsh. Cassidy's black hair lay mussed against her cheek. Her ski jacket was ripped at the pocket, her calm smile replaced with tight-lipped fury. As if to emphasize that, a smear of dark red dashed across her chin.

Blood.

For a moment Ty got sucked into the past, a cross somewhere between Donnie's last moments and the never-ending nightmare of war.

*Please God, not now.*

He pulled oxygen deep into his lungs, then deeper, until they could hold no more. Then he exhaled and brought the world back into focus. Cassidy helped Jack onto a nearby chair. Neither one seemed to notice his space out.

"What happened?" Ty hurried over, helped ease off Jack's coat. The boy's moan did nothing to reassure him.

"Get the first-aid kit from over the sink." Cassidy turned her back, pouring water into a big stainless-steel bowl. She grabbed a clean tea towel and began gently dabbing at what would soon be a glorious black eye. "Ty?"

"Yeah." He pulled the kit off the shelf, set it on the table and snapped open the lid. For once his precautions paid off. He laid out alcohol swabs, gauze pads, ointment, anything he thought they'd need.

Since Cassidy was so totally in control, Ty held back, did as she asked and waited until the last cut was covered.

"Do you need a doctor, Jack?"

"No." The boy glared at him through one eye, holding ice against the other. "I'm fine."

That belligerence got to Ty but he told himself to relax.

"What happened?"

"Someone jumped me."

"Why?"

Jack and Cassidy shared a glance that bugged Ty.

"I asked why."

"They wanted the airplane." Jack's voice shook slightly. "Boe and I were flying it in the yard."

"But I thought—" Ty bit off the words as fast as he could, but it was too late. Jack knew what he'd been going to say.

"I know you said we'd do it together, but you're so busy, Uncle Ty. And I wanted to see how it worked." The boy hung his head. "Boe had to go home early, so I figured I'd give it one last try. I guess that's why I didn't hear them coming."

"How many?"

"Two." Jack burst into tears. "They took it. I'm sorry, Uncle Ty. So sorry. I didn't mean for it to happen but—" His sobs died away. He scrubbed at his eyes. "It was the best gift I ever had and I lost it."

"I'm just glad you're all right." Cassidy hugged him, grimaced when he yelped with pain. "Sorry. It wasn't your fault, Jack."

"Wasn't it?" Ty ought to turn around and walk away, get out of this room before he said something he would regret. He ought to, but sheer anger took over. "I specifically told you to wait for me. But once again, you couldn't follow my directions. You had to do it your way."

Jack glared at him.

"That's not fair," he burst out. "I always do it your way. You say you'll be five minutes and you're three hours. You promise you'll do things with me but you never keep your promises. You always push me to the sidelines because you think I'm too young. I'm not too young, Uncle Ty."

Ty opened his mouth, saw Cassidy's face and reversed course.

"People will begin arriving soon for supper. This is neither the time nor the place."

"It never is," Jack muttered.

"I need to think about this. I'm going to make sure it doesn't happen again."

"How? By tying me up?" Jack looked to Cassidy for support but she remained silent, her pale face troubled. "I didn't cause it, I didn't do anything wrong. But that won't matter, will it? You'll just think up some more rules I have to follow."

Jack lurched from the chair, grabbed his jacket and hobbled across the room. He paused, his voice brimming with hurt.

"Just once, it would be nice if you could look at me and

see me as a competent person who doesn't go around doing lame things."

A moment later he was gone.

"He's right, you know," she said.

"You're taking his side."

"There are no sides here, Ty." One hip against the table, Cassidy crossed her legs at the ankle and her arms across her chest. "You don't treat Jack properly."

Shocked by the comment, Ty frowned. "What?"

"He's a good kid, usually respectful. He gets good grades. He puts up with your excuses and broken promises and not having the life most kids do at his age. But you offer him very little understanding." She bit her bottom lip. "He didn't mean to have the plane stolen."

"I know that. It's not about the plane."

"Isn't it?" She straightened. "I think it's all about the plane. And your brother. And your guilt."

"Playing psychologist, Cassidy?" he mocked.

She nodded, as if she'd expected him to say that.

"Go ahead, Ty. Snap at me. I was walking around the block to get some fresh air. I didn't check with you first. Maybe you should dock my wages or something." Her eyes brimmed with hurt and anger.

"Don't be silly." Why hadn't he stayed upstairs?

"When does it stop? When will you have enough safe-guards in place that you can let go and relax?"

*Never.*

"I'm responsible for Jack. It's not wrong for me to want to make sure he's safe."

"It's not wrong for you to take an afternoon off and go skating with him, either. But you never make the time. Have you asked yourself why?"

She was getting too close. Ty wanted to turn tail and run

but that would only give Cassidy the ammunition she needed, so he pretended what she said next didn't matter, pretended he didn't care what she said or thought, pretended the sight of Jack's battered and bruised face hadn't gutted him.

"You know so much—tell me."

"I think you're scared stiff that Jack is going to turn out like your brother, a runaway who got into drugs and ended his life on the streets." Cassidy leaned forward, her tone daring him to argue. "I think you're so afraid that you'll disappoint Gail that you're putting Jack in a straitjacket of rules so he won't get hurt."

"And here I thought you were just a cook."

She flinched at his snipe but she didn't look away.

"Lash out at me, Ty, if it makes you feel better. Put me down all you want, but please, stop hounding Jack. You're only making things worse."

"You would know. You being his best friend and all." His petty jealousy burbled out from its hiding place, shaming Ty.

"I'm trying to help him. And you."

"By siding with him against me?"

"I'm not doing that." Exasperation echoed in the slap of oven mitts against the counter. "You *were* right about one thing, Ty. I don't have time for this. May I suggest you find a way to get Jack involved in this place? Because if you don't, he's going to look somewhere else for someone who'll spend time with him, someone who won't berate him every time something bad happens."

*Like Donnie did.*

She didn't say it but Ty could read the unspoken remark in the frosty glare Cassidy shot his way before she turned to rescue her casseroles from the oven.

He searched his brain for a way to bring back her generous smile, to wipe out the ugly words he'd tossed at her.

"I'm sorry" was the best he could come up with.

As he climbed the stairs to the roof, Ty whispered a prayer for help.

"I'm pushing everyone away because I'm scared." He watched the sun sink below the horizon. "If running the Haven is what You want me to do, I need help, God."

The words hung in the air like warm breath on a cold winter's morning, shedding a clarity Ty had never seen before.

Maybe God didn't want him here.

Maybe he had it all wrong.

Maybe it was time to admit he'd made a mistake, to call Elizabeth and ask her to find someone else.

Donnie was gone.

But Jack wasn't.

Not if Ty could stop him.

What would Cassidy think?

## Chapter Eight

Multitasking had never come in so handy.

"I did look at it, sis. The location is perfect for the kind of restaurant I want to run." Cassidy held the phone to her ear with her shoulder, using her hands to shape biscuits for tonight's stew dinner.

She listened for a moment, nodded, though no one was in the kitchen to see it.

"I know I should put a deposit on it, but it's only the first of March which means I've got four more months here before I can work on my own plans. And then there's the other thing. I want to make sure that's settled before I go ahead."

Then she kept her mouth shut while her sister sang their reformed father's praises.

"I'm glad you've mended things with him, if that's what you want. But I don't—want that, I mean. I can't forgive or forget that easily, sis. And I sure don't want him back in my life, ruining everything I've tried so hard to build." Cassidy gritted her teeth as the boil of anger festered inside. "Maybe you think he's changed, but I don't trust him."

They talked a few minutes more before Cassidy made an excuse to hang up.

She smacked the dough into a ball, flattened it and stabbed the cutter into it, muttering dire imprecations through clenched teeth.

"Should I come back later?" Ty leaned in the doorway looking as if he'd just left a Mediterranean cruise ship. "I think there's steam coming out of your ears."

"Wouldn't surprise me." The stiffness between them remained. "Something you need? I'm only a humble cook, but I'll do my best to satisfy, sir."

She expected another apology, though he'd already offered many. What she didn't expect was his laughter.

"You are mad. Here." Ty removed his jacket, puffed out his chest. "Take your best shot."

The mischief flirting in his eyes pushed Cassidy off balance.

"What are you talking about?"

"Throw the dough at me. It will make you feel better." He braced his feet wide apart and slung his arms at his sides as if preparing for the onslaught. "Go ahead."

Ty looked positively lighthearted. And extremely handsome. If only— Cassidy broke free of her wishful thinking.

"You've been breathing in too many paint fumes, Ty. You'd better head up to the roof, clear your sinuses." The dig was too hard to resist. He was forever hiding out on that roof.

"Just to be clear—you're refusing to throw that at me, right? Fine." He tilted up his chin in a cocky attitude reminiscent of Red. "But don't think I'm going to give you a second chance. Next time you may have potatoes or eggs nearby."

"And your pretty clothes would get messy, wouldn't they?" she teased, won over by his good humor.

"I do not have 'pretty' clothes. Do I?" He plucked his shirt away from his midsection as if to check for frills. "Blue. Very masculine."

And a great compliment to those gorgeous eyes.

While he pulled his jacket on, Cassidy concentrated on finishing her biscuits. Anything to avoid staring at him.

"How's the sign going?"

Ty paused in the act of pouring himself a cup of her fresh coffee, made a face.

"Not exactly as I'd envisioned. There's paint all over the place, but Jack seems to be enjoying it."

"It was a great idea to have him work with you on that."

"Approval, Cassidy? For me?"

She hadn't heard him move behind her and when she turned Cassidy couldn't avoid meeting his gaze.

"If you're asking if I think you did a good thing by asking Jack to help paint a sign for this place, then yes."

"You mean I actually did something right?"

"You've done a lot of things right, Ty, and you know it. I keep hearing how great you are at helping people figure out problems."

"But not yours, hmm?"

He was too close but Ty didn't seem to think so. He remained in place, sipping at his coffee, watching her in that analytical way that made her uncomfortable.

"I don't know what you mean. Excuse me." She edged past, her heart rate clopping in her ears like horses' hooves racing for the finish line.

Once the countertop was scrubbed down there wasn't anything more to do. The meal was ready. But with Ty hovering she couldn't relax. She poured herself a cup of coffee, added cream. Finally sat down on one of the kitchen stools she kept handy. Ty sat across from her.

"Are you sure you don't want to talk about whatever had

you walloping that dough? Or arguing on the phone yesterday and the day before."

"You were listening?" She felt trapped, cornered.

"Not intentionally." He held her gaze with his soft blue
stare. "You can talk to me, Cassidy. I'll listen." A wry smile
touched his mouth. "I might not be much help but I will listen.
You can trust me."

Trust? It was tempting to unload her fury. But Ty was all
about God and how He cared for those who were His
children. And Cassidy was way past trusting Him. So she
stared into the mocha-colored brew and kept her mouth
firmly closed.

"Is it—er, man trouble?"

The delicacy of his question caught her unawares.

"What?" A hot flush rose as she got the gist of what he was
asking. "I do have man trouble but not from a boyfriend."

"Okay." A curious smile flickered across his face for an
instant, but he said nothing more, simply sat. Waited.

She wanted to trust him. So badly.

"It's personal," she sputtered.

"Problems usually are." He poured himself another
coffee, held up the pot until she shook her head. "What
kind of man trouble?"

"You're very pushy."

"I'm concerned. Jack and I have dumped on you often
enough, I think it's time I reciprocated."

"You were the guy who didn't want to counsel anyone,
remember? Now you're looking for work? Is there a chance
you could just forget it?" She kicked her heel against the
stool leg, hoping her snappish tone would be enough to kill
his interest.

"Not a single chance."

This was the edge of a precipice. If she told Ty the truth,

if she risked showing him the bitterness and anger she'd kept inside for all these years, risked letting him witness that stupid, vulnerable girl, she also risked his condemnation.

And Cassidy did not want Ty to condemn her. But—

She took a deep breath and jumped over the edge anyway.

"My father wants a reunion," she blurted, her stomach churning with disgust.

"Ah."

At least he hadn't judged her.

"I don't want to see him. Ever."

"He must have really hurt you." Ty's expression held no judgment, no surprise, nothing but a welcoming interest.

"Hurt me? He did his best to ruin my life." She couldn't quite stop the venom that oozed into her voice. "My mom wasn't in the grave a day before good old Dad was smashed out of his mind and screaming at us."

"He must have been in a lot of pain after losing his wife." That infuriated her.

"Yeah, a lot of pain. He lost his punching bag."

Ty didn't say anything but a glint of understanding flashed through his eyes and Cassidy knew he understood why she'd been so curious about his comments to Irina on the subject of abuse.

"We girls weren't doing so hot, either, having just lost our mother. But we knew better than to look to him for any comfort. He might as well have died with her for all the good he did us." She expected Ty to frown in disgust, to lecture her for saying such an awful thing. Her sisters had.

But Ty's handsome features didn't alter. "You don't mean that, Cassidy."

"Don't I?" She closed her eyes, exhaled and pretended a lack of concern that simply wasn't true. "I was prepared to forgive him, you know. Years back I could have let it all go, the abandonment, the misery, the lies. After all, I survived, got out. I was making my own way."

"Was?"

Cassidy smiled at his quickness. Ty didn't miss much.

She closed her eyes and in an instant she was back in that shabby upstairs bachelor room, full of high hopes and expectations.

"Go on."

"You may live to regret saying that." She gathered her thoughts and pressed on. "My sisters were almost finished with college. I had enough money saved to pursue my dream. The next day I was supposed to leave for Paris."

"And your dad showed up."

Cassidy would have smiled at his astuteness, but it hurt too much.

"Not when I was there."

"What does that mean?" His brows drew together in confusion. He shifted in his chair, as if to brace himself.

"He learned of my plans somehow. He sat outside my place and waited until I was gone. Then he conned his way inside, went through my stuff and stole my cash, my ticket, everything. By the time I returned, he'd stolen my entire dream."

Ty sat silent, studying her. It was as if he understood she needed time and space to regroup, to collect her composure. Then again, maybe he didn't know what to say about her sorry little tale. Maybe he regretted coming down here now.

"I'm sorry that happened to you, Cassidy." He brushed her shoulder with a gentle hand. "I'm so sorry."

"Aren't we all?" She cupped her mug in her hands and let the steamy warmth caress her cheeks. "I was really sorry when I sat there, in the room I would have to move out of in less than forty-eight hours. I was more than sorry that I was homeless without a dime to pay for a new place. And believe me, sorry doesn't begin to describe how I felt knowing I'd spent years working overtime, weekends, holidays so I could scrape together enough money, and he took it as if it was his. He couldn't even look me in the eye, had to sneak in. Well, I'm not going to be sorry again."

Ty's hand dropped away. A frown marred his good looks. "But maybe—"

She smiled. He was good at listening, yes. Ty had heard. But he hadn't understood.

But then how could he? His home had been happy, his family normal.

"Why are you looking at me like that?"

"It's funny how often I've heard that." Cassidy shook her head. As the strands of hair brushed her face she wished they had the power to wipe out her past. "Maybe he had an excuse that makes it all okay."

"I wasn't—"

"Maybe doesn't help when your sisters are crying because they're hungry and you can't find a thing in the cupboards to feed them, Ty. Maybe doesn't put a present in your stocking on Christmas morning. Maybe doesn't cough up the money you need to go on a school trip with all the other kids."

Cassidy struggled to close the lid on the past.

"My father has not been part of my life since the day he broke into my home. I see no need to meet him now that he feels guilty."

"But—"

Whatever he was about to say, Cassidy didn't want to hear it.

"I'm not going to listen to his tales of woe and say that I understand, because I don't." She crossed her arms over her chest. "I don't understand how any father could do that to his child and I sure don't understand how a so-called loving God could let it happen."

"You can't blame God."

"Isn't He supposed to be all-powerful?" She glared at him, daring him to excuse God's part in this.

"He is." Ty sighed. "Cassidy, you have to see your father sometime."

"Why?" She forced a smile. "That man was never a real father. He wasn't there for me when I needed him. He abandoned us more times than I can imagine. He abused us and my mother."

"And?"

"And now I've abandoned him. I'm free of him, and I intend to stay that way."

Ty frowned. His fingers pleated then smoothed the soft wool of his pants. When he lifted his head, Cassidy glimpsed a shadow in his eyes and knew she wouldn't like hearing what he was about to say.

"But you're not really free. You're carrying around this load of hate." Ty held her gaze. "Sooner or later you're going to have to forgive him so you can move on."

Cassidy jumped up from her stool, winced as it crashed to the floor behind her. She'd trusted Ty, believed he'd understand. But he didn't.

Why hadn't she kept her ugly secrets to herself?

"Forgive him?" Harsh laughter exploded from her. "Is that what the Bible says?"

"Yes, as a matter of fact."

She shook her head. "I will never forgive him."

"You'll have to, if you want to heal." The smug remark rolled out of his mouth as if he'd memorized it years ago.

"That's a crock, Ty. Psycho mumbo jumbo you guys drag out to make people feel guilty whenever they talk about their real emotions." Fury punched out the words. "Anger is an appropriate response. So is bitterness. I'm not going to pretend both of those, which I've felt for years, will be washed away if I hear him say he's sorry. Facing him isn't going to heal me no matter what your Bible says about it."

He rose slowly from his chair.

"Has anger or bitterness helped you, Cassidy?" His quiet voice fell into the silent room.

"They helped me survive, push myself to make my dreams come true."

"I thought Elizabeth did that."

"She provided the opportunity. I grabbed it—who wouldn't? But I made the most of it by focusing on what I had to do."

Ty's hand closed around hers as if to soften his next words.

"Is that why you push so hard here, Cassidy? Is that why you work twice as much as you need to, take on more and more? Because you're over your bitterness? Because you're past your anger?"

"I'm using them to spur me on. I thought you wanted this place to be a success. I thought I was helping." She dared him to deny it.

"Oh, I'm not complaining." Ty smiled. He looked so relaxed—so unaffected—by what she'd told him. "You're making a huge difference here. And everyone appreciates it. But are you doing it because you're committed to the Haven?"

"Why else?" She straightened the stool, glanced at the clock. Anything but look at him.

Ty tilted her chin so she had to look into his eyes.

"Or are you doing it because there's a chance your father may come back into your life and you need to prove that you are worth loving? And you're trying to show him how much he missed out on?"

She'd thought he didn't understand—but how could he know that?

Cassidy grabbed a pair of pot mitts but Ty held her hands.

"Nothing's going to burn so don't pretend. There's always been truth between us, Cassidy. Let's not stop now."

"Fine." She laid down the mitts. "Say what you need to."

"You're blaming God as much as your father. But people are given a choice about their decisions. God can't give us free will and then tear it away every time someone does something you don't like."

"He's supposed to be a God of love," she argued, furious at the lump that wedged itself at the base of her throat.

"He *is* a loving God. Loving someone doesn't mean you force your will on them. It means standing back and allowing them to make their decisions."

"Then what good is it to trust Him, to pray to Him, if He's going to let bad things happen anyway?" She felt like a child saying it, but the question had haunted her for too long. "What's the point?"

"The point is to trust God to see you through the bad times, to be there for you."

Cassidy opened her mouth to respond, but a large crash overhead distracted them both. She glanced at Ty, saw that all color had drained from his face. His hand shook when he reached out to the counter as if to steady himself.

"Ty?"

Several minutes passed before he tore his gaze from the ceiling to glance her way.

"Yes?" Even his voice sounded faint.

"Should we go up and investigate?" No response. "You let Jack use the gym to paint the banner, didn't you?"

"Yes."

"Something might be wrong. We'd better go up."

"Okay." But he didn't move.

Ty's behavior was so strange that Cassidy felt no compunction about grasping his arm and tugging on it to get him to move. But he reared back at her touch, blinked.

"Are you all right?"

"Yes." He turned toward the stairs. "I have a bad feeling."

His feelings were right on.

Paint sprayed across the floor, reaching well beyond the stretch of tarps someone had lain to protect the hardwood. Jack was trying to scoop up red and navy and white paint with minimal success.

"I'm sorry, Uncle Ty. Red and I were talking and then Boe came along and I forgot the cans were behind me and I tripped and—" He stopped, gulped.

Ty's face blazed with anger. She needn't have worried. He was back to normal.

"I can't believe you let this happen. Look at the floor!" He grabbed a nearby roll of paper towel and began swabbing up the paint. "We have to get it off before it stains."

Cassidy directed the three others to pull the corners of the tarps together so the paint stayed inside. Red raced to get a garbage bag from the supply cupboard.

"Go get a mop and a pail of warm water, Jack. Quickly." She worked furiously to clean the paint off, but the old wood hadn't yet received a new coat of varnish, so it absorbed the paint quickly.

"Here." Jack dropped the pail too near Ty, whose beautiful trousers got spattered with water and a few droplets of the paint. "Oh, boy. Sorry, Uncle Ty."

"Sorry doesn't cut it, Jack. I warned you to be careful. I told you that this floor—"

"Stop talking and keep working," Cassidy said loud and clear as a rebellious look flooded Jack's red face as he glanced toward his listening friends. "You can all help," she told the group.

She splashed water on the floor, tossed them some towels.

"What should we do?"

"Use them like blotters. Don't smear the paint," she warned. "Just press a towel on and lift it off. Then start again."

They worked without saying anything more, aware of Ty's forbidding silence. By the time Red and Jack hauled out two garbage bags of ruined tarps and sopping towels, the worst of the paint had been removed.

"It's a mess," Ty muttered, his lips tight with anger. "How could he be so careless? Such a stupid mistake to make."

"Wasn't it you who was preaching to me about the merits of forgiveness not long ago?" Cassidy snapped, glancing at the door. Jack could return at any time and she didn't want him to hear this. "Jack didn't mean to mess up. And there's no harm done. Not really," she countered before he could interrupt. "I heard Elizabeth say this floor should be sanded and resealed. Sanding will remove what's left of the paint."

*I hope.*

Even she could tell the red had absorbed too deeply.

"You're always trying to shield him." Ty's anger glinted in the almost violet depths of his glare. "He's not a child. You said he was old enough to help. I paid a lot for that canvas banner and now it's trash."

"I'll pay for another one out of my allowance." Jack stood in the doorway, his face red. Behind him, his two friends stood listening. "And I'll make sure it looks great. I did a good job on that one, Uncle Ty. Until the paint spilled."

"I think we should get a professional to do the banner." Ty stared at the big spot as if that would make it disappear. "I'll find somewhere else to cut back."

Jack hung his head. "I'm sorry."

"We all are, Jack. You've got to be more careful. You've got homework, don't you?"

"Not very much."

"I think you should get started on it. It's time for Red and Boe to go home."

"Is it okay if I walk them to the door?" Jack asked, his face telegraphing his hurt.

"Yes. But that's it. We're not having anyone visit tonight. Or tomorrow."

"But we're starting March break! I don't have to worry about school."

"Your English teacher told me you haven't read the material for the next section yet. I think that will take some of your time."

Jack stomped out of the room, letting the door slam closed behind him.

Cassidy glared at Ty.

"Why did you do that?"

He frowned. "Because he needs to concentrate on his studies."

"You know what I'm talking about, and it isn't school. Why couldn't you have asked his friends to stay for dinner, let him have the evening with them? Why do you have to be so hard on him?"

"Hard on him?" Ty glared. "We just chucked about four-hundred dollars' worth of paint, signs and tarps because Jack wasn't paying attention to what he was doing. He's got to learn responsibility. What happens the next time he goofs off and something happens?"

"Why do you automatically assume he's goofing off?" She glanced at his pants, knew they were ruined. Add another hundred to his estimate of the damage. "Accidents happen, Ty. To everybody."

"Of course they do. That's why he has to be extra careful."

"He's barely thirteen. He probably feels awkward and un-comfortable most of the time. He's trying to get used to life without his mother. With you. In a new school. You've got to stop pushing so hard or—"

"Or what?" Ty demanded.

He was furious with her.

"Tell me what else I should be worried about, Cassidy."

"I didn't say you should worry."

A picture of Jack two nights ago when he'd sought her out before a cooking class filled her mind. He'd hung around, waited for everyone to leave so he could speak to her. His words still haunted her.

*I think Uncle Ty wants me to go away from here. I think he hates me.*

"I need to tell you something, Ty, but I have to get back to the kitchen. Can you come down there so I can work while I talk?"

He glanced around, shrugged. "Not much more we can do here, I suppose." He followed her to the kitchen.

Cassidy checked the stew, pulled out the biscuit trays. She drained the potatoes and asked him to mash them while she put the finishing touches on the salad. Then when all was ready, she pointed to a chair.

"I need to tell you something. More of my ugly history, I'm afraid."

He nodded, sat, waited.

"When I was twelve, my dad disappeared. By then I was used to it and I'd hide what little money I could so that I could still buy milk and bread. But it ran out and pretty soon we were all very hungry."

She hated saying it, hated going back, digging through the past, exposing the sordid truth. But Cassidy pressed on, because Jack was worth it.

"Eventually a neighbor noticed and called Social Services. They took us away from him and sent us to his sister."

"That must have been a relief."

"You'd think so." She made a face. "It was horrible. Sure, we had enough to eat, we didn't have to worry about somebody not being at home when we got out of school, but it was not an improvement."

"Why?"

"She had rules. Thousands of them. I know she was only trying to protect us but they made us feel like we were always being punished. They also made us feel as if she didn't care about us, as if she was waiting for an excuse to get rid of us." Cassidy inhaled. "We felt like she hated us for interrupting her life."

Ty studied her with a frown.

"You think that's how I make Jack feel?"

She slowly nodded.

"I love Jack, Cassidy. And I don't begrudge his presence in my life."

"I know that."

"Meaning you think he doesn't."

"He's a kid, Ty. He learns by making mistakes." She shrugged. "Yeah, they're messy mistakes and are inconvenient, even annoying. But if Jack didn't act his age he'd be pretty uptight and you'd be trying to figure out how to get him to relax."

"You think I should let him be with his friends."

"It's a school break. He has to do something. What's wrong with having the kids here, where you can keep an eye on them? You've got to cut him a little slack if you don't want to alienate him. The last thing you want is for Jack to feel he's in the way."

Ty dragged his fingers through his hair, heaved a sigh.

"You're right. I overreacted again. I guess because Elizabeth is asking about a grand opening date and I'm nowhere near ready for that."

Cassidy opened her mouth, thought better of it.

"You were going to say something," he prodded. "So say it."

"You and Jack could do something together," she suggested. "Something side by side so that if he gets off track, you can correct it before it goes too far. Just the two of you."

"Any suggestions?" He didn't look as if he relished the prospect.

"Red's always bugging me about learning some recipes. Maybe this is the week to get a teen cooking class going. You can help with that." She laughed at his gloomy face. "'Fraidy Cat. Better get out of here before I put an apron on you."

He nodded but he didn't leave immediately.

"Thanks for sharing," he said quietly.

"If it helps, I'm glad I did. Maybe something good can come out of that misery."

"Will you think about forgiving your father?"

"No. What he did was unforgivable."

Cassidy bent over the oven door and pretended she was too busy to talk anymore.

But when Ty left, the room felt barren, lonely. Like her life.

Yet Cassidy couldn't quite wipe out the memory of Ty's hand on hers, sharing her pain.

Nor could she forget his words about forgiveness.

Or figure out what to do about them.

# Chapter Nine

"This was an awesome idea, Cassidy."

Enveloped in a thick white apron, Jack bore a smear of cocoa above his eyebrow, white icing on his chin and flour in his hair. And he'd never looked happier. Ty quashed a pang of envy, wishing he had the same ability as their pretty chef to bring that joyful smile to his nephew's face.

"They look good. How do they taste?" Ty poked one of the brownies with his finger.

"Eat it and find out." Red glared as if he'd insulted her skills.

He tasted one.

"Very nice." The words barely escaped his lips when the lights went out.

"Everybody stay put," Cassidy ordered. "I've got candles here someplace."

Ty barely heard the words.

"Not again," he breathed as the horror gripped him. "Oh, please, God, not again."

"Ty? Ty!"

*A siren, feet rushing past. Someone calling his name.*

"It's okay. I wasn't hit. I'm fine. I'm fine." He repeated it over and over, willing himself to believe his own words.

"Ty, snap out of it. Come on. We're all fine. It's just a power outage." A hand closed around his upper arm. "Sit down here. You're safe. Nothing's happened."

That fragrance. He knew it. And the voice—quiet but commanding.

Cassidy.

He dragged out every ounce of self-control, shook free of the numbing stupor. Candles flickered all along the counter. The room was empty save for him and Cassidy.

"Jack?" he whispered, wiping a hand against his damp brow.

"He and Red are checking the doors. Mac is upstairs making sure everyone is all right."

"No candles," he rasped, his throat dry and rough as if he'd breathed in a ton of smoke. "No candles up there. Dangerous."

"They have flashlights. Everything's fine."

He leaned his back against the chair and drew in cleansing breaths, waiting for the terror to dissipate. Once he was back to normal, he glanced at Cassidy. Her expression was grim.

"I think it's about time you explained to me exactly what's going on with you."

"I don't like the dark."

"Don't lie to me, Ty. Not anymore. I've asked you several times since I've been here and each time you either ignore the question or fob me off. Tonight you scared all of us. I want the truth."

He licked his lips, searching for a drop of moisture to ease his parched throat. She must have noticed because Cassidy poured a glass of soda and handed it to him. Ty gulped it down. He was always thirsty after a panic attack.

"You're not going to walk away and pretend nothing happened. You've been lying to me for weeks." She glared at him. "I want to know what's wrong with you."

"I didn't lie, Cassidy. It's not something I talk about."

"Until now." Frost edged her voice.

He studied her for several minutes, but deep inside, Ty knew Cassidy would not let him bluff his way through. Maybe it *was* better if she knew the details. Maybe she could ensure nothing bad happened the next time he zoned out.

"There was an—incident when I was in Iraq. Certain things trigger an episode and I relive that time. Technically it's called post-traumatic stress disorder."

"And you chose a homeless shelter to recover from this?" Her gaze revealed her disgust. "Don't you think you should be in a hospital?"

"No. There's nothing wrong with me. Physically, anyway."

"What does that mean?"

"It means I won't hurt anyone or damage anything. I really am fine."

"I said the truth, Ty. The whole truth." She would not relent. "I told you about my father. I've never told anyone that story. The least you can do is be honest with me."

He hated talking about it, hated how it diminished him, made him feel stupid, helpless and incompetent. But this was not the time to hide.

Cassidy was part of the Haven, an important part. She'd poured herself into the project, given unstintingly. She'd bent over backward doing whatever he'd asked of her, gone beyond any expectations in helping him with Jack. If Ty was honest he'd admit she was quickly becoming more than just a co-worker, though he wasn't sure what to do with that knowledge.

"It's not a matter of honesty."

"I think it's completely about honesty. Tell me what happened, Ty."

She wanted the truth? Fine. Let her have it. Then he'd see how she felt about total honesty. He gritted his teeth, forced out the words.

"The attack killed five men. Five men who had come to me for counseling, for help, because they were afraid. Do you know what I told them to do?"

"No."

The knot of disgust tightened inside his gut, forcing out the shame he could not escape.

"I told them to face their fears. I told them to go back out into that nightmare and look their fear in the eye."

He laughed, the irony of it never more razor sharp than now. They'd faced their fear and it had cost them their lives. But he lived with his fear every single day. Fear that he'd give the wrong advice again. Fear that he'd mess up and others would die.

Because of him.

"I relive that afternoon," he told her, unable to mask the wobble in his voice. "I see them preparing to leave, I feel the blast and then—they're gone."

Pity turned her silver eyes gunmetal gray. Her fingers squeezed his shoulder.

"It wasn't your fault. You were doing your job."

"Really?" That painful rasp that hurt his throat could not be called a laugh. "I could have sent them home, Cassidy. I could have scribbled *mental distress* across their file jackets and they'd be alive today. It's my fault they're dead."

Cassidy stared at Ty, her heart racing as he slammed a fist into his palm the same way the truth slammed into her heart.

He hadn't lied to her.

Ty had tried to protect her and Jack from the nightmare that tortured him.

Ty was not a man trying to fool her, but a man desperate to rebuild his life.

Now she understood why Ty hadn't wanted to talk to Irina, why he shied away from others who came seeking his help. Ty didn't want to risk saying the wrong thing again. He'd pushed ahead with everything at the Haven except the counseling part of it because guilt had stolen his confidence.

Armed with that knowledge, Cassidy forgave him. And in the forgiving came healing empowerment. No longer was she a victim of cheating and lying. She was free to stop hiding, free of the fear that someone else would abuse her trust.

Free to reach out, to help a man she cared about.

Ty sat huddled in his chair, his face tortured. Cassidy crouched down in front of him, covered his hands with hers.

"The war, the explosion, the deaths—you couldn't have prevented any of it, Ty. You're not that powerful." Her fingers tightened on his. "In your heart you must know. You went over there, you did your job and you helped as many people as you could. Some didn't make it. But that wasn't your fault."

"I should have sent them home."

He didn't pull away from her touch, so Cassidy stayed still, drawing strength from the shadows around them that allowed the intimacy of sharing.

"Were they medical cases? Unfit for duty?"

The battle for truth played out across his face.

"No," he finally whispered.

"Then you wouldn't have been doing your job if you'd sent them home. The government trusted you to make that call, Ty. And you did. You listened, you used your knowledge and experience and you gave them the best advice you could. You're not at fault."

He studied her for a long time before his fingers tightened around hers.

"My head hears and agrees," he murmured, his breath brushing her cheek. "But my heart wants them back."

"Can't you trust God that they are safe with Him?"

Cassidy wasn't sure where the words came from. She didn't trust God, hadn't since her father had stolen her future. But this wasn't about her. This was about Ty and he did believe. More than that, he trusted God.

"Trust God?" He peered at her through the dimness of the flickering candles. A faint smile touched his lips. "I guess I never thought of it that way. I've been so engrossed in what I feel, hear and see that I didn't—" His voice trailed away as he worked through the issue in his own mind.

Gradually, like an ebbing tide, the tension in his body dissipated. His grip on her hands changed from clinging to something she couldn't understand. It was as if she saw Ty in a whole new light.

Like a movie, Cassidy replayed past mornings when she'd shown up at work only to find Ty huddled over a cup of coffee, face gray, eyes tortured. She remembered the times he'd tried so hard to back out of a counseling session, realizing now it was not because he didn't want to help the people here, but because he did but was afraid his help would do more harm than good.

Like snapshots in a photo album, she saw him with Jack— tentative, cautious, uncertain of himself. And there was Jack, needing someone strong and confident to help him through the doubts. It wasn't that Ty didn't want a relationship with his nephew, Cassidy realized. It was that he was afraid he'd fail him, just as he thought he'd failed his fellow soldiers, his brother.

"Thank you."

Cassidy found him staring at her, his eyes serious but no longer tortured.

"I didn't do anything."

"You did. You made me say it out loud, face it. I've never really done that—not as thoroughly as I did here, with you." He loosened one hand, brushed her cheek. "How did you get so smart about God?"

"I'm not."

"You are. All this time I've been putting my faith in myself, in how I could handle things, how I would manage, as if I'm God. But I do believe God is in control of the world. I need to do my part and let Him do His." He touched her nose with his forefinger. "You reminded me of that. Thank you."

"Oh. Well, you're welcome." His nearness made her nervous. She tried to pull away, to distance herself, but he wouldn't let go of her other hand, and stood up with her. "Instead of hiding away, going through these episodes alone, why don't you give the rest of us a chance to help you? You should know talking sometimes diminishes the strength of your reactions."

"Okay. I'll come find you next time and you can soothe my fears away."

It wasn't the hint behind his words that made her warm, it was that look in his eyes, the way his fingers squeezed around hers.

"Would you kiss and make it better, Cassidy?"

Transfixed by the mesmerizing stroke of his thumb against her cheek, Cassidy froze; a deep yearning billowed up inside her. She didn't know what to do next.

She didn't have to decide. Ty leaned forward and kissed her, the light brush of his lips sending shockwaves through her body. The connection between them had been born the day she'd met him and simmered beneath the surface ever since.

So Cassidy leaned into the kiss, lifting her arms to circle his neck, burying her fingers in the tendrils of hair that curled against his nape. His hands moved around her waist and he drew her closer, intensifying the embrace until she could think only of him.

As quickly as it had begun, it was over. For a moment, Cassidy couldn't understand why. She blinked, wincing at the harsh glow backlighting Ty.

The power was back on.

Embarrassed, she dropped her hands, then stepped back so his fell away from her.

"Cassidy?" His fingers pushed against her chin, forcing her to look at him. "Are you all right?"

"I'm fine." She glanced around to avoid his stare. "Look at this mess. I've got to get it cleaned up."

Ty said nothing as she blew out the candles, ran the dishwater and began wiping up the baking mess. After a minute, he began washing the dirty cooking utensils.

Silence hung awkwardly between them, but Cassidy couldn't think of a way to break it without sounding girlishly silly. It was just a kiss, after all.

"Everything's cool upstairs," Jack told them, bursting into the room with Red at his heels. "What are you doing with our brownies?"

"Putting them away so they don't dry out. Do you want to take some home, Red?"

"I wouldn't mind." She accepted the plastic-wrapped tray greedily. "I wish you'd do this more often."

"What? Bake?" Cassidy forced herself not to stare at Ty. Her heart rate accelerated at his disheveled hair, mussed shirt. Had she done that?

"Yeah, bake." Red frowned. "You give those women classes about how to cook. How come you can't teach us?"

Cassidy blinked her surprise. It was the first time Red had shown interest in any program at the Haven. "You want to take cooking lessons?"

"Yeah, but not with those women. They know too much."

She'd be surprised. But Red's words sparked an idea she'd

had weeks ago. Cassidy had so much else going on that she'd left it perking in the back of her brain. Maybe it was time.

"Thursday evenings work for me. Seven to eight-thirty."

"You mean you'll do it?" Surprise filled Jack's brown gaze.

"Starting this week if you can find five more kids who are interested."

"Not a problem." Red grinned.

"All right!" Jack beamed.

"Cassidy." Ty stood behind her.

The tone of his voice warned her he wasn't thrilled.

"It's a good idea, Uncle Ty. I know a lot of kids at school who have to fend for themselves when their parents are working. If they knew how to cook some simple meals for their brothers and sisters, don't you think that would be good?"

"I think it would be wonderful, Jack. But Cassidy's already doing something almost every night of the week. It's a lot to ask of her."

"I'm only here until June. I don't mind squeezing in a few extra hours if it will help." Cassidy caught Jack's triumphant glare at his uncle, saw worry crowd Ty's beautiful blue eyes. "But only with your uncle's permission. I know it's a liability to have kids working in the kitchen and you probably have to check with Elizabeth about insurance and all that stuff."

"Yes, I do." Gratefulness gleamed in his gaze. "I also need permission slips from the parents agreeing that their children may take the class. I can make up a form tomorrow morning." He turned to Jack. "Will that be a problem?"

"Permission slips? Like in elementary school?"

"It's what the board requires, Jack. I am their employee, after all."

"Yeah, I know." He looked to Red. "Think they'll go for it?"

"They'll go for it." She grinned. "Thursday evening. You're on. I'll spread the word. Thanks for the grub." Then she was gone.

"I'd better finish my reading." Jack left with two brownies.

Suddenly they were alone in awkward silence.

"Are you sure about this, Cassidy?" Ty's concern filled her with joy. "You're making a meal every night but Sunday. You've got brunches, lunches and classes. I don't want you to burn out."

"I'm having too much fun to burn out." What a dumb thing to say after that kiss. "But I do need part of tomorrow afternoon off. I asked Irina to cover, and she's fine with it if you are."

"Of course." He waited expectantly, but Cassidy couldn't tell him about her errand. Not yet. "Take all the time you need."

"Thank you. And thanks for the help. We're done here."

But Ty didn't go. He kept watching her. The funny fidgety feeling inside ballooned.

"I guess I'd better call a cab," she murmured.

He cleared his throat.

"Um, if you're not in a hurry, I thought you might like to come up to the roof."

The roof? She was invited to his private place?

"I'll get my coat and meet you at the stairs."

Ty left. Cassidy filled her lungs with air, told her heart to calm down.

"Just because you think you can trust him, don't go getting gaga."

Her heart ignored that.

"It's a perfect night," Ty said, meeting her at the stairs.

Perfect for what? Cassidy didn't ask. Instead she followed him to the roof. He closed the door behind them and switched off the light.

"Look up."

Cassidy blinked, surprised by how different the city looked from up here. She peered into the night sky, saw stars sprinkled across the sky, glittering against the dark backdrop.

"It should be a good night to see Mars." Ty revealed his telescope.

"That's what you've been doing up here? Stargazing?"

"It's more like communing with God for me." He peered through the lens, found the spot he wanted and adjusted the controls. "Take a look."

Cassidy didn't know what to expect. Telescopes had never been part of her life. She'd never even wanted to peer through one before. But one look and she was transfixed by a soft red glow.

"It's Mars." Ty stood beside her, slightly behind, his body acting as a shield against the chilly spring breeze. "Can you see it?"

"Yes." She could also see and hear and feel him, very near, murmuring facts and figures about the night sky. *Concentrate.* "Why is it so foggy in some places?"

"Pollution or space dust. Mars is highest in the sky between now and two o'clock. That's the best viewing time."

Ty was so close that his breath warmed her cheek as he moved the telescope slightly to show her different stars.

"It's beautiful." The magnificence awed her.

"It was created by God, all of it designed from a master plan. Isn't that remarkable?" He grinned. "I get chills sometimes, just thinking about such creative genius."

Cassidy had never thought of God as a genius.

"Humans prize imagination, but what kind of mind must it have taken to design our solar system and stars with nothing to go on? I think that's why I was so moved when I went to the Middle East. At one time, it was the cradle of civilization. They have artifacts all over the place marking the history of generation after generation. And God was there the whole time."

"You really believe that?"

"I *know* that. Don't you?"

Cassidy thought about it for a moment.

"We used to go to Sunday school when we were kids. Mom would haul us out of bed, clean us up and we'd walk the five or six blocks to church. God always seemed more like a judge to me, a taskmaster." She smiled at her memories. "Some of the sermons had me shivering in my shoes."

"The Bible does talk about God's anger against those who abused His goodness or wouldn't obey," Ty agreed, snugging her jacket around her neck and pulling the zip all the way up. "Better?" He waited for her nod. "But there are wonderful passages about how much He loves us, how far He'll go to keep us. His infinite patience is what I admire most."

"Why?"

Ty laughed.

"Probably because I have so little. I can't understand how God could even want the children of Israel when they kept complaining in the desert. I mean, they had food, they had water and they weren't slaves. They whined because nothing was familiar—but the very thing they were trying to escape was familiarity."

She searched her brain for some memory of the Bible and came up blank.

"Later on God told this prophet called Hosea to take a wife, Gomer, who kept getting involved with other men. Repeatedly God orders Hosea to bring her home." He brushed his knuckles against her cheek. "It's a perfect illustration of God's patience and love toward us."

Cassidy shivered in the night breeze, grateful when Ty hugged her against his side.

"Why did Hosea have to marry a woman like that?"

"To show that He chooses people who are, in themselves, nothing out of the ordinary. It's what He chooses to do with those people that makes the difference. Should we go in? Are you too cold?" His tender voice chased away the chill.

Someone would interrupt them if they went inside. Or she'd be too embarrassed to ask questions. Here in the dark it was easier to forget her uneasiness, ask when she didn't understand and revel in being with him. She shook her head.

"Go on."

"Gomer kept being unfaithful, it wasn't just a one-time deal. So for Hosea to keep bringing her back must have made him look stupid to the community. But God was trying to teach His people that His love doesn't die because they do something wrong. So He insisted Hosea restore Gomer as his wife over and over."

"She must have been quite a woman."

Ty grinned.

"That's the amazing part. She wasn't an unusual person. Neither was Abraham. God didn't owe either of them anything, they deserved nothing. And yet God chose to bless them both because He wanted to show His love."

"I've never heard that part of the Bible before." Cassidy felt silly saying it. She wasn't a heathen; she'd been to church. But she'd never read those passages.

"It's there. In the Old Testament. Book of Hosea. The gist of the entire book is about pursuing our own personal agendas instead of doing what God asks."

"I don't understand what that means. Oh." A star shot across the sky in an arc that flared then dissipated. "We went to church when Mom took us."

Ty continued, "That's good, but there are lots of reasons for going to church. For some, it's a way to socialize. Not to learn about God, but to meet and greet, to be seen or make business contacts. As if going to church means you can be trusted."

"My dad should have gone. Maybe—"

"Going to church doesn't make you any better than the guy

who goes to his service-club meeting every week, Cassidy."
He led her to a bench, waited till she was seated, then pulled
a blanket he'd brought over their legs. "Lots of people go
because they think they'll lose status if they aren't seen in their
regular pew."

His nearness distracted her from the questions that were
filling her brain.

"Why do *you* go?"

"The reason I should be going is to worship God, and to
learn what He asks of me. What I shouldn't be doing is
going through the motions. That usually means I'm trying
to make God into what I want, instead of figuring out who
He really is."

"I think of God as a stern judge," she admitted, edging a
bit closer.

"Who punishes you because you did something wrong?"
He smiled at her nod. "So you've made God into a judge. Lots
of people think God is like a grandfather, spoiling them, not
making them follow the rules."

"I never saw God as a grandfather."

"Some people call Him a 'higher power' and talk about
tapping into Him. Essentially they mean God is there to serve
them. That's what Hosea the prophet was supposed to preach
about. Gomer was the picture of those people."

"Oh."

"Read the story for yourself. We can't pursue our own
interests and ask God to pitch in when we need Him."

Cassidy frowned. She didn't like that. And in her mind, it
didn't make sense. If God *was* God, then He had everything.
And if He loved people so much, why wasn't He willing to
help them out? To punish those who misused them?

"You're so quiet. Have I confused you?" Ty smiled at her
nod. "Don't be afraid to ask questions, Cassidy. You told the

students that tonight. Because it's the only way to learn. Not that I have all the answers. But the Bible does."

"I don't understand what the problem was."

"The problem was God's people were putting themselves first." He pushed a strand of hair from her eyes. "They ignored and distorted God in the process."

"How?"

"Same as us. God is the only thing that will satisfy. We keep trying our own methods to find happiness. We think God owes us and we blame God when things don't go the way we want."

Cassidy looked away from his piercing gaze, afraid he could see straight into her heart.

"We have to learn to trust God even when we don't get our own way." He grimaced, shook his head. "You need to study it yourself."

"I see." What did she know about studying the Bible?

"There's another month-long study on Hosea they're running at the church. I just finished it. You could give them a call, register for a session."

"I'll think about it." She needed time alone to consider what he'd said, to read the passage for herself. Cassidy rose. "It must be late. I'd better get home."

Ty checked his watch, clicked his teeth.

"And I was going to get Jack in early tonight. But thanks for sharing Mars. I always enjoy looking at the red planet."

*I enjoy being with you.*

But Cassidy didn't say it.

Instead she thanked him, then hurried downstairs while he covered his telescope. She summoned a cab and left before they could meet again. But even with the fire burning, her cozy little cottage didn't seem as comforting tonight. A thread of discontent unraveled inside her, making her want more.

Cassidy studied the drawing of her dream restaurant, one she hoped to run one day. She'd hung the sketch on the wall as motivation, to keep her focused on her goal. As she looked at it now, she wondered why it didn't seem quite so bright, quite so enticing.

Her conversation with Ty clung to the back of her mind. She debated a moment, then dug through her storage trunk and pulled out the tattered copy of the Bible she'd received one Christmas. She couldn't find the Book of Hosea, so she used the directory at the front, then thumbed through the thin, rattling pages until she came to the passage Ty had described.

Slowly she read, trying to align what Ty had said with the words on the page.

It didn't all make sense and Ty's comment kept returning. *We think God owes us.*

Ty seemed to think that was wrong thinking. A few weeks ago Cassidy would have debated that.

Now she wasn't so sure.

Maybe it was time to figure out exactly what she could and couldn't expect from God.

## Chapter Ten

With March break over and the kids back in school, Ty had expected the pace at the Haven to slow down.

Wrong.

The place was busier than ever. Spring seemed to bring everyone to the old brick school, and a lot of those visitors came through his office door.

He'd hoped the flashbacks and nightmares would diminish, that Cassidy was right and talking about them would help ease their powerful effect.

He'd been wrong there, too.

The weight of dread increased each time a client began talking about their problem and looked to him for help. The nightmares came almost every night now, fracturing his sleep, attacking his confidence. Ty struggled to push through the fear; he faced every situation praying desperately for relief.

And through it all he kept a desperate watch on Jack.

At the moment, Jack was helping Cassidy launch a new mom's cooking class. The kid was a natural teacher. After Cassidy showed how to create a grocery list from a menu, Jack explained different cooking terms. Ty had intended simply to stop by, but he couldn't tear his gaze away from his nephew, who looked a totally different boy, or from Cassidy, whose glowing face constantly filled his mind. When she called for a break, Ty couldn't leave.

"He's good, isn't he?"

"I've never seen Jack so engaged. When did this happen?"

"He's been helping me out, and it gave him confidence." She grinned, raised her shoulders in a shrug. "Now there's no stopping him."

Cassidy had done for Jack what Ty should have.

"How did your session go?" she asked.

"I suggested a marriage counselor."

"Oh." She looked disappointed. "You couldn't help?"

"They need specialized treatment, but even then, I'm not sure either of them is willing to work through their issues. Neither have fully committed to making their marriage work."

"But they're married. They have children."

"They've made all the outward moves toward commitment. But in actions and thoughts they are still individuals. A specialized therapist could help—if they go."

"Selfishness."

"Pardon?" He couldn't stop thinking about how beautiful she looked.

"Selfishness. I've begun to realize that it's at the bottom of so many problems. I keep seeing it over and over. Kids, parents, wives, husbands. We're all pushing so hard toward our own goals." Cassidy made a funny face. "Me included."

"What do you mean? You give way above and beyond."

Her expression grew pensive.

"But do I do it because I want to get my six months over with? Or do I do it because I want to help? I keep asking myself that."

"Anyone who was just serving time would hardly be here

every night, long after their 'duty' was over." Ty touched her arm. "Is something going on? Do you want to talk about it, Cassidy?"

"Yes, I do," she said, surprising him with the firmness of her answer. "But not right now. Could we meet later on the roof?"

"Sure." Ty had longed to spend more time with Cassidy, but he wished it didn't have to be during the one moment he'd set aside to pray for confirmation of a decision he now realized was imminent. "I'm just heading up there now."

"It's not dark yet. You won't be able to see anything." She nodded toward Jack. "Why don't you stay for the rest of the class? Jack would appreciate having you here. He doesn't get to see much of you lately."

Cassidy's gentle reprimand hit home. Ty had been avoiding Jack for the past few days. They'd managed to get along without any big blowups, and Ty was afraid of ruining that.

"He needs your encouragement, Ty. Your being here would be good for him." Her sweet smile coaxed him to agree.

Ty couldn't refuse when she looked at him like that. He remembered their kiss.

"I could stay for a while. What are you making?"

"Lasagna." When he licked his lips, her laughter lilted up to the ceiling, bringing a smile to the ladies' faces. Even Jack grinned. "Don't worry. I'll make sure you get some when we're finished."

"I hope so. I need to keep up my energy." Ty rolled up his sleeves and stepped up to a nearby table. "Do you ladies mind if I join you?"

They didn't. Soon the room was brimming with the robust aroma of tomatoes and oregano. Ty felt utterly inept as he stirred the bubbling sauce, trying to avoid the scalding droplets that burst up and out of the pot.

"The burner's too hot, Uncle Ty." Jack flicked the switch.

"Simmer means a really low heat. And if you don't move the spoon so fast, it won't splatter you."

When Jack dabbed a red splotch from his forehead, Ty's humiliation multiplied.

"Thanks."

"Cassidy says nobody knows everything. We all have stuff to learn." Jack moved on to show one of the women how to lay the noodles in her pan.

In some ways the class was a fiasco. The ladies asked him to pour the sauce over their noodles but Ty couldn't seem to manage the big pot without splashing all over himself. He was pretty sure the best cleaner in Chicago wouldn't be able to save his shirt.

Jack had a good laugh when Ty skinned his knuckles on the cheese grater, but because it wasn't the familiar sneer Ty usually saw, he was able to join in and laugh at his own ineptitude. For the first time in a very long time, it felt like they really connected.

Until Red and the gang appeared in the kitchen doorway at the end of the class. Ty struggled to hang on to his relaxed attitude. After they greeted Jack in some kind of weird salute, whispered together, Ty's tension inched upward.

"They're going for a soda. It's just two blocks away. Can I go, Uncle Ty? I won't stay long, I promise."

A picture of Donnie feathered through Ty's mind. What if—

Every sense screamed at him to say no and to get Jack home as fast as he could, away from these negative influences. But he'd promised Cassidy he'd talk to her and he'd promised himself he'd push past the fear and allow Jack a bit of freedom.

"One hour," he said, checking his watch. "And don't be late, Jack."

"I won't." Jack grabbed his jacket then followed his new friends out.

"He'll be okay," Cassidy murmured at his shoulder.

But she couldn't guarantee that, and they both knew it.

The ladies insisted on cleaning the kitchen, so Ty led Cassidy up to the roof. They spent a few minutes peering through the telescope, but clouds had rolled in making it difficult to see. Ty didn't mind; he wanted to hear what she had to say.

The roof looked different tonight. Low lighting revealed a variety of shapes, left enough room to move around but didn't glare or blaze. He breathed in the rich perfume of flowers. A quick glance around revealed a row of cedars in massive pots. In front of them were chairs, his benches, a table or two. Scattered around the space were planters just beginning to bloom.

"You did this," he said, seeing the truth splashed across her lovely face.

"Davis and the guys helped when you went out this afternoon."

"It's beautiful."

"I hope you don't mind. The name of this place is the Haven and since this seems to be your haven, I thought it should be a little more comfortable. Davis put up an awning that extends from the roof so you can even sit up here in the rain."

"It's fantastic." He had a good look at everything, but when Cassidy perched on the edge of a loveseat, he knew she was more troubled than she'd let on.

*Please God, let me be a help. Don't let me freeze up.*

"What did you want to talk to me about?"

Cassidy lifted her head.

"I've found the place I want to rent for my restaurant."

"Restaurant?"

"Yes. It's in a fantastic old building."

He blinked, surprised by the passion in her voice as she told him of her lifelong dream. When she was finished, Ty could almost see the place in his mind.

"The picture—on your wall. It's of a restaurant, isn't it? Your restaurant."

Cassidy pressed one raven strand behind her ear as she always did when she was deeply engrossed, as if that strand broke her concentration. She wore a different perfume tonight. Fuller bodied, hinting at facets of her character he had yet to discover.

The thing was he did want to know them. All of them. In fact, Ty wanted to learn everything he could about this amazing woman.

"Tell me."

"A friend drew that sketch after I described my dream restaurant. I keep it hanging there to remind me of my goal. But lately I've been wondering if my dream is ever going to become reality."

"Why? Have you changed your mind?" He winked. "You want to stay on at the Haven, is that it?"

"You wish." She laughed, but he caught an inflection of pain. "I've really been enjoying my time here. I never thought I would."

She stared into the night. A frown marred the smooth expanse of her wide forehead.

"Cassidy?" When she didn't answer, Ty wrapped an arm around her shoulder. "Talk to me."

"It's my dad, again." She made no attempt to move away from Ty's arm.

"He's written me a letter asking me to forgive him."

"And have you?"

She twisted her head to peer at him. Teardrops hung from her dark lashes.

"I can't," she whispered, shaking her head from side to side. "I wish I could. I'd like to put it all behind me, to pretend it doesn't matter. But it matters, Ty."

"Of course the past matters. But—"

"If I could say the words and make all the pain and damage magically disappear, don't you think I would, if only to be free of it all?" She scrubbed at her wet cheek like a little girl who's embarrassed about crying in front of the neighborhood boys.

Ty trapped the tear dangling on the end of her long lashes with a fingertip. "But the hurt goes too deep?"

She nodded, sniffed.

"I can't say that I forgive him, because I won't mean it and I refuse to lie." She hiccuped a sob, blew her nose and straightened her shoulders. "He left us alone, Ty. We were just kids. He promised me he'd come back that night, but he didn't. He abandoned us as if we were no more than stray cats. We could have died in a fire. We could have been attacked or worse and he wouldn't have even known. Probably wouldn't have cared."

"Don't say that."

"It's true." Bitterness laced her aching voice. "We needed a father. But all he ever worried about was where the next drink was coming from. His own children and he couldn't be bothered to love us."

"I'm sorry." He drew her head against his chest and let her weep out the pain that had built up over the years. "I'm so sorry, Cassidy." Ty brushed his lips against her glossy black head, closed his eyes at the silken touch. "I wish I could say something that would erase it all and make you forget."

A few more sobs escaped before she drew slightly away, dabbing at her tears.

"What do I do now? I don't want to write in words that I can't forgive him. I don't want to put that down in black and white and send it to him to read. It would be almost as bad as what he did to us. But—" She sighed. "I want him to leave me alone."

"It doesn't sound like that's going to happen. This is the second time he's contacted you, isn't it?"

"Actually it's the fourth."

*Fourth?* He blinked, shocked by the knowledge that she hadn't said a word.

"This is his third letter. He contacted my sisters, got their forgiveness and moved right back into their lives."

The bitterness in her words made him ask, "But not yours?"

"No. Not mine. I'm not saying he's not sorry. Maybe he is. But it isn't enough."

There was something else. Ty began to probe, hoping he wouldn't hurt her too deeply by digging into the past.

"Tell me what it was like at your aunt's, Cassidy."

She caught her breath, stared at him. "What do you mean?"

"You said there were lots of rules. What else?"

"I took care of my sisters. I made sure their clothes were clean, that they had school lunches, that they didn't bug her when she had her card group over." Cassidy drew in a shaky breath then continued. "I made sure they did their homework. On the weekends, to give her a break, I took them to the library or we'd go to the park and I'd read to them."

"How old were you?"

"When we got there?"

He nodded.

"Almost fourteen."

Almost Jack's age. His heart ached for the girl who'd tried so hard to protect her family.

"There are two years between each of us. My aunt lived about two blocks from where I live now. We went back with my dad a couple of times, but he always took off and we'd end up with her again."

"Did your friends know?"

"At school?" She shook her head. "There was no time to play with anyone after school and when we were in class, it didn't seem to matter. We all had problems. Ask Davis."

He would. Ty wanted to learn as much as he could about Cassidy.

"When you finished high school? What did you do then?"

"I got a job. Two of them, actually. I cooked in a hotel dining room and I ran a little catering business on the side. My aunt agreed that my sisters could live with me. They both won full academic scholarships to college." She said it proudly, as if she were their mother. "One's a physiotherapist. The other is doing her surgical residency."

"You didn't want to go to college, like they did?"

She shrugged. "I didn't have the money. But I could cook and I loved it and people paid me well. At Christmas I made a killing catering staff parties. I scoured the cookbooks in the bookstores and memorized a new recipe each time I went in. Pretty soon I ad-libbed my own. Pastry came easily to me, so I specialized."

"You are an amazing woman, Cassidy Preston."

She frowned. "I did what I had to. There wasn't anything heroic about it."

He was amazed she didn't realize how much she'd accomplished.

"So you went to Paris?"

Her face transformed into a bitter mask.

"I almost didn't. I scrimped and saved for ages. And then *he* broke in and stole it. I think that's what I can't forgive. Or the fact that God let him do it."

"That's why you're mad at God." He saw the truth on her face. "It doesn't help you, Cassidy. You've clung to your anger and bitterness for years, but none of it makes you feel any better. Even when he's come asking you to forgive him, it isn't enough."

"I know you think it should be." She drew away from him. The distance was like a cool wind that blew between them.

But Ty wouldn't give up. He wanted to help. Maybe he'd

say the wrong thing again. Maybe he'd do more damage than good. But he could not walk away from this woman and leave her wondering why God didn't care about her.

"What if you told him what you're feeling?"

"God?" She frowned, half shook her head. "I don't think—"

"Well, telling God isn't a bad idea, either. But I was talking about your father. What if you told him how badly his actions hurt you?"

"No. I don't want to see him. I'll get all mixed up and the words won't come out right. He'll talk me into something and I don't want that." Her hands knotted together as she edged forward on the seat.

"Then write it down." Ty crouched in front of her so she had to look at him. "Write your father a letter, Cassidy. Say everything you want, tell him exactly how you felt when he abandoned you. Tell him how it felt to come home and find out he'd stolen what you'd worked so hard to build. Write it all down."

"He won't like it."

"You're not doing it for him, you're doing it for yourself. To heal."

"Then what?"

This was the hardest part.

"Then you tell God you need to find a way to forgive your father." Anger rushed in to darken her features but Ty hung on to her hands. "You told me he promised he'd come back."

"Yes."

"But he never did that."

She almost vibrated with anger, silver eyes dark as a storm cloud.

"That lie has hidden in a corner of your heart and festered for years. It's why you blame God. Because He abandoned you when He didn't bring your dad home. Am I right?"

"Yes." She hung her head.

"Dear Cassidy, God didn't abandon you. He was right there, waiting to comfort you. He sent you Elizabeth to make sure you realized your dream."

"Why didn't He stop all our pain?"

"I don't know. I only know He had your best interests at heart and that He's been waiting all this time for you to let Him heal you. But you have to ask Him, Cassidy. You have to be willing to let go of the poison of unforgiveness."

"I can't."

The plaintive whisper broke his heart, but Ty couldn't stop now.

"You can, Cassidy. You're a strong woman. You make a decision and you push forward to achieve your goal. You protected your sisters, you did what you had to but now, you must end this bitterness or it will eat you up, ruin the years you have left." He pushed the dark strands away from her face so he could see into her eyes. "Don't you want to be free?"

"Yes." Emotion gushed out in that simple word.

"Then take charge. Don't let hate and anger control you anymore. Say what you need to in your letter. If you need time, tell your father that. You're in a position of strength, Cassidy. What happens next is totally up to you."

Doubt fluttered across her face, but eventually she nodded, freed her hands and pushed her palms against her cheeks and back, drawing away the tear tracks from her cheeks.

"Thank you." She smiled, rose, offered him a hand to pull him upright. "If you ever need a professional reference, I'll give it. You're very good at drawing people out."

"I only tried to help. It hurts me to see you suffer." Ty moved close enough to tip his head forward and press his forehead against hers. "Your mother must be very proud of you, Cassidy Preston."

He angled his head and brushed his lips against hers. It was a fleeting kiss, asking no deep questions. And she was still wrestling against the barrier she'd erected between herself and God. He'd pray about that.

Cassidy drew away too soon. She didn't look at him as they left the roof.

"Jack must be back by now."

Except he wasn't.

The hour was long gone and Jack had not returned.

"I should never have let him go." Ty paced the foyer in measured steps that did little to quash the knot in his stomach. "What if he's hurt?"

"He's just forgotten the time," she soothed.

"He can't afford to forget it," Ty snapped, then apologized. "I'm sorry, I—"

They both froze at the sound of laughter outside. A car door slammed outside. A moment later, Jack burst through the door. The pleasure on his face drained away as he caught Ty's glare.

"I'm sorry. We went for a ride and—"

"A ride? In a stranger's car? You said you were going for a soda two blocks away. You promised you'd be back in an hour."

"But I—"

"No excuses, Jack. Riding in cars without permission is not allowed." That's how Donnie had started. Riding with friends. Drugs. Then he'd run away. "You know the rules."

"I know that I can't do anything. I'm a prisoner here. You want to control every inch of my life."

"You two need to go home," Cassidy interrupted, tilting her head toward Mac, who was halfway down the stairs, watching them. "There are people upstairs trying to rest."

"Yes, you're right. We'll drop you off on the way." Ty handed Jack the backpack he'd carried down from his office. "Let's go."

Jack flopped into the backseat, his face rebellious. Cassidy sat in the front but she didn't remain silent for long. She shot Ty a look then twisted in her seat toward Jack.

"I raised my two sisters, when they were about your age." Her face tightened. "If they'd pulled what you did tonight, I'd have grounded them for a month."

"I didn't do anything wrong."

"Not true. Do you know how I felt, standing there, wondering why you broke your promise, afraid something had happened to you?"

Cassidy was furious. Her fingers curled around the edges of her handbag leaving her oval nails pale in the glow of the dash lights. Her mouth pinched tight, her eyes narrowed, darkened.

"I'm sorry, Cassidy."

"Don't be sorry, Jack. Keep your word. I thought I could trust your word. I hope I wasn't wrong."

Ty pulled up to the curb in front of her house. He reached for his door handle but she stopped him.

"No. It's late. You're tired and you need to get home. Just wait until I'm inside, please?"

"Of course. Good night. Remember what I said."

"I will." She climbed out. A moment later she'd disappeared inside her house.

"She was really mad." Surprise colored Jack's voice.

"She was really scared," Ty corrected. "We both were."

"But why? I wasn't doing anything wrong."

"Yes, Jack, you were. You made a promise and you didn't keep it. You have a cell phone but you didn't call to ask if you could go in that car. I trusted you. We both did. And you let us down."

For once Jack had nothing to say as they drove to the rooms they shared, the impersonal place that had never been home.

Ty was glad of the silence. He needed to think about finding someone else for this job. Someone who didn't have a family to protect.

Only, how could he walk away from Cassidy? She'd taken root in his heart.

## Chapter Eleven

For three nights Cassidy struggled to put her feelings onto paper. For three nights she stopped when the hurt grew too big. She was afraid it would never go away.

But today, this last day of March, was her thirtieth birthday and she was determined to get it done. Yet every time she started writing, she remembered Ty's touch, his kiss, the tender way he'd held her. Almost as if he—loved her?

*Get a grip.*

Was she so needy that she couldn't accept friendship for what it was?

*Focus.*

Cassidy grabbed another sheet of paper. If she was going to make it to church this morning, and she was, she had to finish. The study in Hosea had cleared her thinking about God. Not that she understood why her father had done it. She didn't.

But she now realized she had to accept that God loved her, that He would do what was right. Her job was to trust.

*Dear Dad:*

She poured her heart onto the page without holding back.

If it hurt him to hear, she was sorry. But Ty was right. She couldn't keep pushing everything down. It was time to get rid of the past and move on.

Cassidy felt almost empty as she wrote *I forgive you*—as if a giant weight had been lifted away. It was over. The needy little girl who cried for her father's love was all grown-up.

But Cassidy couldn't quite suppress the fear as she signed her name. She'd bared her soul, told her father about the dream he'd ruined, explained that she still intended to make her dream of owning a restaurant come true.

What if he tried to sabotage that, too?

The doorbell rang. She stuffed the letter under her notepad to mail later. Then she grabbed her jacket and her bag and hurried to open the door to Ty.

"Hi." She couldn't stop smiling at him.

"Hi, yourself." He held her jacket so she could slip her arms into the sleeves. His eyes widened as she straightened her narrow skirt and he caught a glimpse of her new sandals. "Wow!"

She giggled, curtsied. "I'll take that as a good wow."

"You should. You look great."

"Thanks. Shall we go?"

"Yes." He waited till she'd locked the door then guided her to his car with a hand against her waist.

Cassidy blushed at the burst of joy she felt at his touch.

"Hey, Cassidy. You look hot."

"Hot?" She frowned, checked her face in the visor mirror and caught Jack's grin. "Oh, thank you. What's with all the books?" A stack of texts littered the backseat.

"Science paper. It's due before Easter. I forgot to take them in."

"Easter's only a couple of weeks away." Cassidy couldn't stop staring at Ty's long, capable fingers as they gripped the wheel. A few days ago, that same hand had cupped her cheek. If she closed her eyes, she could still feel his touch.

"Are you listening, Cassidy?"

She jerked back to reality and Jack's voice.

"So me and the guys have to come up with something by tomorrow."

"Any ideas?" Ty asked Jack, shooting her a knowing smile.

"None." The boy flopped against the backseat, arms crossed over his chest. "Science isn't my favorite subject."

"Then it's lucky for you that you have an uncle who's pretty knowledgeable in that area."

Ty frowned at her. "Me?"

"Uncle Ty? What does he know?"

"Quite a lot, as it happens. Especially about astronomy." She ignored Ty's shaking head. "Maybe if you asked him nicely he could help you out with your project."

"I'm not sure—"

"I'll have to ask the guys."

At least Jack hadn't said no. Nor had Ty. Yet.

The little church was not like the big cathedrals Cassidy had toured in Paris. It was like the church she'd gone to as a child. There was nothing stately or elegant about the shabby woodwork with its dents and marks. Nothing finely crafted about the plain wooden pews or the rough-hewn pulpit. But the people were delightful. Some of them were familiar faces she'd become acquainted with at the Haven, some she'd met during the Bible study on Hosea. Most of the grinning faces made her feel at home.

Jack joined the band, happily strumming his bass as everyone sang. The drummer was too fast and the pianist hit many wrong notes, but nothing seemed out of tune.

Instead, joyful voices rose in praise and put the focus right back where it should be, on worshipping God. For the first time in many years, Cassidy was able to open her heart and feel that touch of love fill every needy crevice, mending the hurts until she felt whole and strong. And loved.

The service came to an end too soon.

"You look as if you enjoyed yourself," Ty commented, sliding his hand over hers when they exited into the foyer. "You're a beautiful woman, Cassidy."

"Hey, Cass." Davis's big, beefy arms wrapped her in a bone-crushing hug. "Good to see you here. It's about time."

"Hi, Davis." She returned his hug, then greeted his wife and children.

Ty declined Davis's invitation for lunch, then, holding Cassidy's hand, he led her outside, into the sunshine. She didn't mind a bit.

"You told him we had other plans. Do you mind sharing what those plans are?"

His blue eyes sparkled beneath the hank of unruly hair that flopped over his brow.

"An afternoon at the Adler Planetarium." He nodded toward Jack, who was loping toward them, his guitar case banging against his knee. "After all, aren't you the one who said I should help Jack with his science paper?"

"I thought it would be a great opportunity for the two of you to do something together, and for him to see a different side of you."

"That I'm not such a dud after all, you mean."

"I've never thought you were that, Ty." She tried not to grin with delight when he slid her arm through his and led her toward the car. "You and Jack need to meet on some common ground that has nothing to do with the Haven. Astronomy could be it."

"Did you hear me playing, Cassidy?" Jack's expectant gaze sought hers.

"I sure did. You're fantastic. I expect to hear you on the next karaoke night, Jack."

"Really?" A smile pushed away his usual grumpy look.

"Really. Now what would you say to a hamburger and fries—my treat?"

"Hello, hamburger and fries." He hooted with laughter at their groans and climbed into the car.

Ty held the car door for Cassidy as he explained his idea for the afternoon. "Does that fit your plans, Jack?"

"I guess I could go."

Ty closed Cassidy's door, walked around the car and climbed inside without saying a word. But he tilted an eyebrow at her when Jack began talking about the red planet.

"Thanks," he mouthed silently.

She blushed, and returned Ty's smile.

Jack peppered Ty with questions during lunch, then bounded into the planetarium with the most enthusiasm Cassidy had seen in weeks.

She couldn't help feeling a sense of pride as the two heads, one a sandy brown, one darker, shaggier, bent together in animated discussion as they toured the exhibits. Jack and Ty had finally connected and it was obvious Ty was enjoying his nephew.

"We've got just enough time to see the last show in the star theater," she told them.

The room had filled up quickly and they couldn't find three seats together, so Jack sat across the room, leaving Ty and Cassidy to sit together.

"I'd say you've had a great afternoon."

He snuggled her hand in his. "Thanks to you."

"I didn't do anything."

"Right." He studied her, his gaze probing, intense.

Cassidy returned the look, her heart singing as she realized she loved him. For the first time she was finally able to love and trust someone. But not just anyone. Ty. He'd been honest with her. He didn't steal or lie. He was worthy of loving.

He was a man her heart could cling to and never be disappointed.

But did he love her?

The lights dimmed, the show began. Cassidy heard every word, but she couldn't concentrate. She was too aware of Ty next to her, holding her hand. Perhaps that's why she knew the moment something went wrong.

In the blackened room, a blast of sound vibrated against the floor. Then a glittering white explosion flashed above them. But Ty wasn't watching it. His eyes were tightly closed, his lips clamped together. He didn't make a sound but his hand tightened painfully around hers; his body stiffened.

"It's okay, Ty. It's Cassidy. You're not there, you're here with me," she whispered in his ear, sliding her free hand up his cheek, to cup her palm's warmth against it, hoping to draw him out of the flashback. "It's just a show. Everything is fine."

She kept whispering, though some of the other patrons tossed her an inquisitive look.

"Relax now. Breathe."

He didn't say anything or open his eyes, but the slowing rise and fall of his chest reassured her that he'd heard. She kept touching him, kept steady contact with the warmth of her hand against his icy face until at last the lights went up and the theater emptied.

His pasty gray face worried her, but not as much as the tremble in his fingers.

Ty rose but drew immediately away from her, waiting as she exited in front of him from the row, from the room.

"That was awesome." Jack's grin faded a little when he caught sight of his uncle's face. He glanced her way, opened his mouth to say something but quickly closed it when Cassidy shook her head.

"Maybe you should take a look in the gift shop," she suggested. "Ty and I can have a coffee while we wait."

"Okay."

They set a time and place to meet. Jack hurried off to shop. Cassidy purchased two cups of coffee, then led Ty to a seat behind the famous sundial on the northern lawn, overlooking Chicago's lakefront.

"Have a seat."

Ty sat on the grass, accepted and sipped the dark brew, but remained silent.

"Are you all right?" she asked at last.

"Fine. Sorry to embarrass you like that."

"You didn't embarrass me."

"Right." He'd closed himself off, blockaded the warm, generous man she'd come to know behind an icy mask.

"What's wrong?"

"My life, that's what's wrong." He drained his cup, set it on the grass, then leaned back on his elbows, studying the glittering water in front of them for a long time before twisting his head to study her. "I've been praying for healing for such a long time."

"Healing from the—attacks?"

"If that's what you want to call them." A tinge of bitterness colored his words. "I'm beginning to wonder if I'll ever be free of these nightmares."

"Don't give up, Ty." She slipped off her jacket to let the water's breeze cool her. "Sometimes healing takes a long time, but it's always in God's time."

He frowned, then held his hand over his eyes to shade them, as if he needed a better look at her. Cassidy blushed.

"I know it sounds strange to hear me put healing and God

in the same sentence, but that's how I feel, healed. Free." She plucked a blade of grass, twizzled it against his neck. "I don't think I'll ever be truly able to forget my past or trust my father again, and I know there will be moments when I slip back into my old way of thinking, but I forgive him."

"Oh, Cassidy. I'm so glad for you."

"Writing it down was the turning point, I think. Putting everything on paper—" She glanced at him. "How did you know?"

"I didn't. Just a guess."

"I doubt that. Or if so, it was a very astute one. Very therapeutic, too." Cassidy let the sandal dangling from her toe slip off onto the grass. "It was great at first. I twisted the tap and all the venom came spouting out."

"Toward your father?"

"Dad and God, both. I'd been bottling so much up. But each time I'd try to finish the letter, I'd end up rewriting it. Some of the things I put on paper were really awful, hateful things. I saw myself in a new light. It wasn't pretty."

"What do you mean?"

"I had my plan all worked out. When I'd saved the money, bought the ticket, was ready to go, my plan was coming together."

"And then it didn't."

"Yes." Her stomach lurched but Cassidy refused to dwell on it. The past was over. "I was furious that the God of the universe hadn't followed my plan. Who did He think He was, anyway?"

Ty chuckled.

"When I think about it now, I see myself utterly consumed with my own importance. I got so far off the track, so self-centered." Cassidy winced. "It's no wonder I thought God had abandoned me. There was no room for Him in my life."

Ty gazed out across the water, wearing the troubled look she'd seen so often.

"I thought counseling was what I was supposed to do," he murmured, when the silence had become unbearable. "People told me I was good at it. I certainly enjoyed it and thought God was using me over there."

"What makes you think He wasn't?"

He twisted to glare at her, fingertips messing up his hair in an act of pure frustration.

"I caused three men's deaths."

"Did you?" She frowned. "I thought an incendiary device did that."

"Yes, but I feel responsible."

"How you feel doesn't mean it's the truth." She held out her finger, hoping the butterfly that had been circling them would land. "I've learned feelings fluctuate wildly."

Ty's eyebrows rose. An explosive heat moved up Cassidy's neck and scorched her cheeks. She ducked her head, but refused to back down.

"Believe me, if it seems strange to hear me talk this way, it feels even stranger to say it. But it doesn't change the truth. God is who He is—omnipotent. That means He's in charge. You're not." She lifted her head, met his stare. "Something bad happened. And it bothers you. But that doesn't mean you stop doing what you're supposed to."

"Which is?"

The words flowed out without conscious thought. It was her heart speaking.

"You're a natural counselor, Ty. You don't bully, you don't even press very hard, but you do have a way of getting people to face their own personal truths, to challenge their validity and to move past them." She touched his shoulder. "That's a gift. It might be hard for you to use it right now, but that doesn't mean you should stop. Those people who come to see you at the Haven need you."

"I fade in and out sometimes." The admission cost him. Shame filled his eyes. "They'll be sharing something that's very important to them and one of the construction workers will drop something and bang! I'm back there—reliving it all over again. It's not fair to the client."

"Has anyone complained?" She did what he'd done so often to her when trying to make her to face a truth. She thrust her forefinger under his chin and pushed up so he had to look at her. "Has anyone asked you not to talk to them anymore, to forget about them and their problems?"

"No," he admitted. "But I want to do more. I want to encourage them, to help them figure out the root of their problems. And all I can do is sit there and let them talk while I fight off the fear."

"They talk, you listen. Isn't that what counseling is all about?"

He growled beneath his breath.

"Tell me what you're thinking, Ty. I can take it."

"Anybody could sit there and listen." His anger spilled over onto her. "I'm supposed to do more than that."

"Anybody? Well, if anybody could do it, why do they come to you? Why do they sit outside your door, waiting until you have a free moment, when anybody could hear their sad tales?" A rush of sweet love poured into her voice and Cassidy could no more stop it than she could hurt him.

"But—"

"No buts. What you do is a gift, Tyson St. John. A God-given talent that brings hope to the hopeless and challenges those who've almost given up to try again. Don't talk to me about not doing anything when your very presence in that office brings help to people who were afraid to ask."

"I'm not doing my best," he whispered. "If only I could get past this stupid stress thing, if God would heal me, there's so much more I could—"

"Did it occur to you that God hasn't healed you for a reason?"

He frowned.

"No, I've never considered that. I came to the Haven to—"

"Make Gail's dream come true. And raise Jack. And take on the problems of the world." She squinted at him. "Your efforts are focused on other people and that's noble. But is making Gail's dream come true part of God's plan?"

She was going to add to that, but caught sight of Jack sauntering across the lawn toward them followed by Red, Boe and two other members of the gang. Ty followed her gaze, groaned.

"How did they get here?"

Cassidy saw a look pass between the kids. She slid her feet into her sandals as worry feathered up her spine. "More to the point, *why* are they here?"

"I'm afraid to ask." Ty rose and held out a hand to help her up, held her jacket so she could slip her arms in the sleeves.

"Thanks." She stayed exactly where she was, not minding a bit when his hands rested on her shoulders.

"Hey. I got a book." Jack showed them a thick, beautifully illustrated book on the solar system.

Her warning system hid red alert.

"They didn't give you a bag?"

*Please, God,* she prayed, *let my suspicions be wrong.*

"Uh, yeah. Sure they did." Jack glanced toward Red, then at his uncle. "I, uh, I guess I must have tossed it."

If he only knew how guilty he looked.

Cassidy snuck a glance at Ty, knew he'd caught the scent of something wrong. Her heart ached for his disappointment.

"Looks expensive." Ty accepted the book, began paging through it. "Eighty dollars. I didn't know you had that much cash left this late in the month, Jack. I mean, you bought that guitar stand and stuff."

"I, um, that is, I had to borrow from Boe."

Ty closed the book, studied his nephew.

"Boe's walking around with a hundred bucks? Where'd he get that kind of money?"

"A hundred?" Jack licked his lips. "You said eighty."

"Boe's hiding a book under his shirt. Red's had her hands in her pockets for too long." He pinned Jack with his gaze. "I'm guessing nobody paid for what they took." Ty handed the book back. "Come on."

"Where are we going?"

"You're going to return the property you stole."

"No!" Jack's face paled so much the tiny scar left over from the day he'd broken the mirror stood out in stark red relief. "They're closed, anyway."

"They have a big function tonight. I'm guessing someone will still be around." Ty's lips pinched together. "I notice you don't deny stealing it."

"They've got lots of stuff. They're not going to miss a couple of things." Belligerence twisted his mouth. "And I'm not taking it back."

"Yes, Jack, you are." Ty's voice got very quiet. "I will not be an accessory to theft. I run a homeless shelter. How do think it will go down with the police when they learn my nephew steals?"

"Who's going to tell them?"

Ty said nothing, simply pointed to the small camera on a nearby post.

Jack paled even more. But he didn't back down.

"I'm not going back there like some four-year-old who stole a candy." His indignation carried over to his chums, who muttered their agreement.

"You're not keeping something that isn't yours." Ty remained silent for several moments before murmuring, "You know your mother wouldn't have allowed that, Jack."

Jack looked toward his friends, but it was clear Ty's words had affected him.

"Come on. I'll go with you. We'll pay for it together."

"I'll wait over there." Cassidy pointed to a bench farther up the walk, watched them walk away together. Jack wasn't saying anything but Ty was.

"What a wimp!" Red snapped her gum. "No way do I want a wuss like that in my group."

Time for a few truths. Cassidy was rusty—her sisters had long since grown up—but she whispered a prayer for help as she faced the audacious girl.

"You don't think it's wimpy to steal kids' toys?" She directed a knowing glare toward the girl's bulging jeans pocket. "You're supposed to be a leader, Red. I thought you were smarter than this."

"Than what?" Red demanded, hands gripping her hips.

"Smarter than shoplifting. I thought you said you wanted a career with kids. Who's going to hire someone with a record for shoplifting?"

"I don't have a record, chef."

Red's sneer made Cassidy's palms itch but she pressed on.

"You will have one if you keep this up. Today you're stealing trinkets. Tomorrow you'll be hotwiring cars, pulling bank heists, knocking old ladies over the head for their pension checks."

Red's fury spilled out.

"I would never do that!"

Cassidy shrugged.

"That's what they all say. But violence starts somewhere, and it usually starts small." She studied the girl. "I thought you cared about the people in your neighborhood." She'd infused her voice with just enough disrespect to grab Red's attention.

"Nobody from around here lives in my 'hood," Red scoffed.

"How do you know? The lady who was working the store—she's working on a Sunday afternoon instead of being home with her family. How do you know she doesn't need every cent she earns to feed her family? What if your stealing on her watch cost her the job she can't afford to lose? What if the security guard has to pay for your crime?"

"He should. He's lousy at his job."

"He's fifty years older than you, at least." Cassidy shook her head. "But because you don't know them personally, you think it's all right to cause them trouble. You're shortsighted, Red. You don't consider the consequences."

Boe and the other two were studying the girl, as if they were seeing faults in Red that they'd never seen before.

"I consider the future plenty. In my house, you have to or you wouldn't survive."

At last, the opening she needed.

"Then how come you didn't consider the fact that Ty and Jack might be forced to leave?" Doubt flashed across Red's face. Cassidy pressed on. "I guarantee boards of foundations like Elizabeth Wisdom's do not like scandal. The behavior of the nephew of the Haven's director will matter if the media get hold of it."

"They won't."

"Because you said so? Right. And we all know how much experience you have—so much that you get kids who are younger than you to commit crimes. Nice gang you have going, Red. Something to be proud of, huh?"

"What do you know about my world?" Red's fury spilled out in a rush of gestures and angry words. "You floated over here from Europe, you had everything given to you. What do you know about anything?"

"Is that what you think? That I'm some kind of spoiled rich kid?" Cassidy laughed at the image. "You're not as bright as I gave you credit for, Red. You judge without knowing all the facts."

Cassidy walked over to the bench, sat down and pretended to ignore the group.

Not many minutes later, Red sauntered over, flopped down on the bench.

"So?"

"So."

"So spill it. Dish the dirt."

"Pardon?" Cassidy pretended confusion.

"Will you tell me about yourself?" Red amended several moments later accompanied by a huge sigh. Boe and friends stayed where they were, shuffling uncertainly. "Which stylist on the Magnificent Mile is responsible for that chic haircut? And that suit—I'm guessing Michigan Avenue?"

"Wrong on both counts. I got my hair cut by your neighbor. She charges me twenty dollars." Cassidy then explained her wardrobe.

"Garage sales? Are you kidding me?"

"Garage sales in the right area," she corrected. "And don't sneer. Sometimes the price tag is still hanging on the dress. My sisters and I worked our way through high school and had to look good on not much money. It's possible, you know."

Red peppered her with so many questions, Cassidy lost track of time. By the time Ty and Jack returned, the afternoon had cooled and then sun was on its way down. But the chill wasn't off the water.

"Can we give you a lift back?" Ty asked, his face showing no emotion as he waited for Red to make the decision.

"It'll be pretty tight, but we wouldn't mind."

The ride home took forever, or so it seemed to Cassidy. Ty remained stoically silent, while Jack, though subdued, forced laughter at the others' jokes. By the time they reached the Haven, Cassidy's head ached. She knew from Ty's pallor that he must be feeling the same.

"Thanks for the ride." Red, Boe and the others high-fived Jack, muttered something about meeting up later. Then, after one glance at Ty's face they shoved each other out of the backseat, hurrying away as if afraid he'd lecture them.

"There will be no get-together tonight, Jack." Ty leaned forward, looked directly at his nephew. His voice brooked no argument.

"Big surprise. I suppose you'll be drafting up another list of rules, too." He shook his head in disgust, climbed out of the car. "I'll go talk to Mac while you take Cassidy home. I'm sure the two of you must have lots of things to talk about. You don't need me."

Before Cassidy could protest, Jack slammed the car door then sauntered up the stairs and inside the red brick building, which now hung a professionally made banner that looked nothing like Jack's creative effort.

She frowned. Jack's tone had carried a hint of—jealousy?

Ty rested his head against the wheel. He inhaled very slowly, then pulled back.

"I'm sorry the afternoon was ruined." Tiredness ached through his voice.

Cassidy guessed he hadn't slept last night.

"It wasn't wasted."

He raised an eyebrow at her, disbelief etched across his face.

"I mean it. I got to have a nice long chat with Red. Very…informative."

"I can imagine."

"How did you make out at the store?"

"He's not allowed in the building for a year. They almost called the police. I managed to talk them out of it, though I'm not sure that was wise." Ty turned his head to look at her. "He doesn't seem to get that what he did was wrong."

"He gets it. Jack's not stupid."

"Then why did he do it?"

"I think he got talked into it and he didn't know how to get out of the situation, or he didn't have enough confidence." She fell silent as he negotiated the streets toward her house. "I think he resents me."

"You?" He laughed mirthlessly. "Jack adores you. You're his poster girl for perfection. He can't stop talking about you."

"Really?" Cassidy preened a little. "I've never been a poster girl for anything." She caught his droll look and blushed. "He finds it easy to talk to me."

"He certainly doesn't find it easy to talk with me. In fact, most of the time, he seems like he can't stand me." Ty pulled up in front of her house, switched off the engine. "I'm not sure my decision to take on the Haven was the right one."

"Don't get discouraged, Ty."

"Discouraged?" He laughed. "I'm a little beyond that today."

"Why? It was a stupid thing for him to do, but I think Jack's learned his lesson."

"Maybe too late." Ty tilted his head back as if to ease some soreness in his neck. "The manager at the planetarium store took my name down, threatened to contact Elizabeth's foundation about Jack's actions. Apparently an expensive kit is missing and they suspect Jack passed it off to the others. Since Jack didn't return it with the book, the guy was very angry. He even threatened to call the newspapers and name Jack as the ringleader if he didn't bring back that kit."

"What did Jack say?"

"That they didn't take it." Ty met her gaze. "What else would he say?"

"Maybe it's the truth. Maybe someone else stole it."

"Yeah. Maybe."

"Please, let things settle for a day or two. God brought you this far. He's not going to abandon you now."

"No."

Cassidy heard no assurance in the word.

"I'll take whatever flack I have to, protect him the best I can. Raising Jack is my responsibility."

"But?"

"But I won't allow our actions to negatively impact the Haven."

"Meaning?" A sense of foreboding filled the car and it wasn't due to the onset of night. Cassidy shivered. She wasn't cold, but Ty's voice, the way he said that— "What are you saying, Ty?"

He shook his head, smiled.

"I'm not saying anything. I have to think things through, that's all." He touched her hand, smiled. "But that's not your worry. You've been great, Cassidy. You listened to my troubles, spoke up to Jack, even took on Red. Thank you."

"I didn't do anything but be a friend." She hoped he'd say she was more than that, but Ty only smiled.

"A very good friend," he murmured. Then he leaned forward and kissed her.

Before Cassidy could respond, he'd pulled away and was opening the car door.

He walked her to the house, waited till she'd unlocked the door.

"I could throw together a sandwich, if you wanted to stay for supper."

"Thanks, but I think Jack and I need to spend the evening at home. It's so busy during the week that there isn't much time for him."

"Anytime," she told him. "Don't give up, Ty. Not with Jack. Keep trusting God. I do."

"I'm glad for you." He studied her for a moment, sighed. "I have to go. See you tomorrow?"

"Of course."

Cassidy stood in the doorway watching, until the taillights disappeared down the street. She flicked on the lights and went inside. After a light supper, she turned on the television for a while, but the face she kept seeing was Ty's.

Cassidy flicked off the television, closed her eyes.

"I trust You, God," she whispered. "Or at least I'm learning to. Tomorrow, I'll mail the letter to my dad and wait for You to tell me the next step. Your will be done. Is it Your will for me to love Ty? Because I do. Please, please, won't You help him? And Jack?"

She sat there a long time, waiting for God's peace to fill her heart. When it didn't come, Cassidy found her Bible and reread the promises she'd underlined in red.

*The Lord your God is with you,*
*He is mighty to save.*
*He will take great delight in you,*
*He will quiet you with His love,*
*He will rejoice over you with singing.*

She repeated the verse over and over until spring's dawn pushed its way into the room.

Ty was sincere, trustworthy and honorable. Now she understood the strange connection she'd felt with him on that first day. She'd waited, she'd watched, and he'd proven to be a man she could love.

Cassidy believed God would heal Ty.

God had allowed her to learn about love from a man who gave it freely, a man who wasn't afraid to open his heart to those who were hurting. A man willing to put his own life on hold for an orphaned nephew. A man she could trust.

If only Ty could love her.

# Chapter Twelve

"Hi, Peter. Nice of you to return my call, even if it is two days late."

Ty tilted back in his chair, cheered by the sound of his college roommate's voice.

"I never return calls on April Fool's day. Anyway, I'm a new papa, remember? Spare time is hard to come by."

Congratulations given, Ty waited for his old friend's counsel.

"I did some checking as you asked. The shrinks who specialize in working with kids are of the same mind as me. Get the boy out of that situation. I know you wanted to make Gail's dream come to fruition, but Jack clearly is at a vulnerable age and has to come first."

"Yes." It felt so good to confide in someone who knew the details of his past and understood his fears. "Jack's already moved on from shoplifting. Yesterday his teacher contacted me about vandalism at school. She insists Jack's involved."

Peter whistled. "He's going down the wrong road fast. How is it between you?"

"I'd thought we were doing better. He's been bringing some of his buddies up on the roof to get my help on a science project they're doing." This was so hard to admit. "I just don't seem to have what it takes to be a parent, Pete."

"Most of us get on-the-job training when they're too little to talk back. You got tossed in with no warning. Don't be too hard on yourself. My friends say he's at a bad age."

"I'm not sure it's just the age. He seems to hate me."

"I'm sure that's not true."

"Jack flouts every rule I make. He's rude. Even Cassidy can't seem to make him see reason lately."

"Cassidy?"

Ty explained about the woman who filled his heart.

"She's had a great relationship with Jack, always seemed to be able to reach him when I couldn't. I was pretty jealous of that for a while. But now he's pulling away from her, too. It's a tough area, Pete, and there are lots of temptations. I'm afraid for him."

Silence, then…

"For him, Ty? Or afraid the past will repeat itself and you won't be able to stop Jack from self-destructing, the way you couldn't stop Donnie?"

"Both," he admitted grimly.

"Then you have to get him out of there."

If only Ty could. Cassidy was here. They'd just begun to explore their relationship. Ty didn't want to walk away from her.

But Jack was his primary responsibility.

"If you were teaching the kid science, I'm guessing you're still hooked on astronomy. That's good. How's the PTSD?"

"Not good."

"Still the flashbacks, nightmares? You're startling at loud sounds?"

"All of that and then some."

"You're under too much stress, Ty. Your brain needs to relax."

"Not so easy to do right now."

"It could be if you'd come into practice with me."

"Join your practice?" The idea intrigued him.

"Why not?" Peter began listing benefits. "There are lots of private schools in New York that specialize in reining in kids like Jack. You could set your own hours, gradually move back into practice. And you'd have the option of selecting your own clients. Nothing too stressful or demanding at first."

"Military school might work." A noise in the hallway caught his attention. Ty called for the person to enter. When no one did, Ty returned to his conversation. "Where would we live?"

"Easter's coming up. Why not fly out here, look around and see what's available."

"I can't. Our grand opening is on Easter Saturday. That's less than two weeks away. Elizabeth is coming, and I want everything perfect for her. I'm going to be snowed under."

"What about right after that? Get everything up and running, find a replacement and then make your move?"

"Find a replacement?" Anyone could do his work. Ty hated handing off Gail's dream, but Jack was more important and getting him away was the best option. "I wouldn't have a clue where to look for somebody to take over the directorship of this place."

"I might. I've got an in with some college profs. I'll see if they know anyone who might be available to step in."

The more Peter spoke, the better Ty liked his idea.

But at the bottom of every scenario there was Cassidy.

"You could set up a practice in Chicago, but it would be too easy for Jack to connect back with those kids, and you'd have to build up your client base. You could walk right in here."

"It's very generous of you, Pete."

"Actually, you'd be doing me a favor. I'm turning people away because of my hospital work. Think, pray. Toss it around with Jack. You're always welcome here, Ty. You know that, right?"

"I do now. Thanks, Peter."

A few minutes later, Ty hung up the phone feeling more hopeful than he had in weeks.

New York. His own clients—he'd be able to stick to what he knew instead of offering temporary fixes to situations so desperate it seemed no amount of counseling could help.

There was still Cassidy to consider, but her goal was to open a restaurant. Surely she could do that as well in New York as in Chicago?

Private school would free Ty from those miserable confrontations with Jack. The boy wouldn't like it, of course. But they would be someone else's rules and someone else would dole out the punishment. Eventually Jack would realize it was for his benefit.

Who was he kidding?

Ty needed to get out of this place as much, or more, than Jack did.


Something wasn't right.

Cassidy had fended off the feeling for the past three days, ever since the debacle at the planetarium, but the feeling persisted, a cloud of apprehension that seemed to hover over the Haven.

She flicked open her ringing cell phone.

"Hi, Elizabeth. No, I haven't put a deposit on the space yet. I can't explain why. I don't understand it myself. It's as if something is holding me back from committing."

Jack wandered into the kitchen. She smiled, waved a hand and pointed to the tray of chocolate-chip muffins.

He nodded, flopped down on a stool, but didn't immediately attack the food. That shocked Cassidy. She tried to concentrate on her conversation.

"I still have almost three months here. To tell you the truth, I'll hate to leave. I love working here. Starting up my own restaurant—I don't know. It seems like a dream, while the Haven is real and very satisfying."

Closer examination of Jack's face told her something was wrong. Cassidy cut short the conversation, promised to call that night.

"Hey, honey. Tough day?" She poured a big glass of milk and set it in front of him, then poured herself a cup of the tea she'd just made. When he didn't answer, she pulled her stool closer to his. "Talk to me, Jack."

"I got an A on my proposal for my science paper."

"All right!" A surge of happiness billowed inside. "Your uncle is going to be thrilled."

"Is he?" Jack kept looking at her, as if he was willing her to see something.

"What do you mean? Of course he will. He'll be thrilled if you ask him for more help."

"I don't think Uncle Ty cares much about what I do, as long as I don't make waves." Jack dunked the muffin three times before part of it broke away and plopped on the table. "He's got all this stuff about the grand opening going on. And you, of course."

Cassidy frowned.

"What do you mean, 'and me'?"

"He'd rather spend time with you than me any day of the week. Not that I blame him." Jack's grin flashed for an instant. "I'd rather spend time with you than him, too."

He'd meant it to be flattering, but Cassidy didn't feel glad. All she'd wanted was to bring the two closer together, yet somehow she'd managed to get between them.

*Help me, God.*

"I like being with both of you. You're my two favorite men." Cassidy hoped he'd smile, but Jack didn't.

"I can take care of myself."

What did that mean? She opened her mouth to ask him but Jack was already at the door.

"Library. See you later," he called before he disappeared up the stairs.

Something really was wrong.

Cassidy finished her preparations for the evening meal with a heavy heart. But then she remembered she wasn't alone and did her best to leave the problem in God's hands. What else could she do?

She'd hoped to discuss Jack's nonappearance at dinner with Ty, but when the last helper had left for the night, neither uncle nor nephew had appeared. She went looking for Ty and found him on the rooftop.

"Hi." Her heart gave a bump of excitement when he twisted away from the telescope, smiling as if he was happy to see her. "I brought you something to eat and a drink."

"You didn't have to." Ty peeked under the foil covering, grinned. "But I'm glad you did. Thank you." He leaned over and brushed his lips against her forehead.

"You're welcome."

"I don't know what I'd have done without you all these months, Cassidy. You've kept me going, cheered me up, pushed me to try harder, aim higher. I couldn't have asked for anyone better to work with."

She curtsied.

"Thank you, sir. Right back atcha." She sat down beside him on the bench, watched as he began eating the taco salad she'd prepared. "That sounded a lot like a farewell speech."

"Wasn't meant to. I just realized how seldom I say thank you." He complimented her on the food. "Are you leaving now?"

"Pretty soon. I thought I'd carry those down when you're finished. Mac and the new guy you hired seem to enjoy each other."

"Uh-huh." Ty stared straight ahead. He seemed far away, as if he wanted to be alone.

But Cassidy couldn't ignore her misgivings.

"Jack didn't come for dinner."

"Probably out with his buddies." Contempt laced his voice. Ty set aside the plate, tasted the dessert then left it, also. He rose, walked over to the telescope. "He'll come back when he's ready and not one second before."

"But—aren't you going to look for him?"

"I have a job to do here, Cassidy. I can't run off every time Jack doesn't show up."

"You're not working now," she pointed out.

He wheeled around, stomped across the roof and glared at her.

"No, I'm having a break. I started at five-thirty this morning. I got called away during lunch and I had to schedule another counseling session for Irina and her husband during dinner. I think I'm allowed to spend five minutes alone, without having to sort out someone else's problems, aren't I?"

Stunned by the seething anger underlying his words, Cassidy picked up the dishes.

How could his words hurt so much? "I'll leave you alone."

She'd almost made it to the door when she felt his hand on her arm, his whisper next to her ear.

"Don't go, Cassidy. Please?"

"I don't want to intrude."

"You're not. I'm sorry. Please stay." Ty took the tray of dishes from her and set it down, grasped her shoulders and turned her to face him. "I didn't mean to hurt you, truly. I'm just—in a foul mood. I'm sorry."

"It's okay."

"No, it isn't." He pushed the hair from her face, cupped her chin in his palm and bent to press his lips against hers. "I'm sorry," he kept whispering between kisses.

Cassidy wound her arms around his neck and returned his kisses, reveling in the love that poured freely from her heart. She didn't have to guard it, she didn't have to be afraid he'd hurt her. Ty was honest and trustworthy. He wouldn't fail her.

"It doesn't matter." She pulled back to study his face. She noticed how thin he'd become, the fan of lines around his eyes, the pronounced jut of his cheekbones. "I love you, Ty. I want to help if I can. Don't shut me out."

He stared.

"You love me?"

"Very much. I never knew I could love anyone this much."

He smoothed her eyebrows, traced a line down her nose and over her lips. Then he kissed her again.

"I love you, too," he told her, his voice clear and rich. "I think I loved you that first day when you started making your list."

"You were furious at me," she corrected with a laugh. He loved her! Her heart nearly burst with joy. "You thought I was too bossy."

"I thought you were perfect," he insisted. "You dug in, got on with your job and made me realize I was sitting back, not doing my part. I couldn't have done it without you, Cassidy. You've made everything fun and interesting and worthwhile. You cleaned up, put things in order and took over this place—including my heart."

Cassidy reveled in his embrace, delighted with the way he was opening his heart to her. Evening darkened as they huddled together, sharing hushed whispers and loving words. Soon twinkles of light appeared above them.

"There's the North Star."

"Ah, you remembered." He snuggled her against his side, pointed out Pleiades, Orion's belt, Cassiopeia. "It's so clear tonight. Too bad Jack isn't here to see how they lie across the sky."

Jack.

The worry returned, nipping at her conscience. What if he was in trouble? What if he wasn't at the library?

*I trust you, God. You are in charge.*

"Cassidy, I need to tell—"

The door flew open, crashed against the wall. Mac stood in the doorway, breathing heavily.

"Ty, you have to come. The police are on the phone."

Ty's arm dropped from her. His face turned to granite as he rose slowly.

"Police. What do they want?"

"They have Jack in custody."

"I'm coming." Ty stepped back so Cassidy could precede him down the stairs. He dragged the door closed and locked it behind him. In his office he picked up the phone, said his name and listened. By the time he hung up his eyes were stone cold.

"What is it? Is he hurt? What happened?" she demanded.

"He was in a car." The words dropped from Ty's lips like ice cubes. "Driving. He hit another car. He will be charged."

"Oh, no." Cassidy reached for his hand but Ty stepped back, out of reach.

"I have to go."

"I'll go with you."

"No."

Cassidy jerked back, stunned.

Ty must have seen how his words impacted her for he reached out, patted her cheek with icy fingers. His perfunctory smile didn't reach his eyes.

"Thank you, but it could take a while. Go home, Cassidy. Try to get some rest. We have a little over a week to prepare for the grand opening, and I know you've got a lot to do. Don't worry about this. I'll handle it."

"Don't worry?" She grabbed his arm, holding him back so he couldn't leave. "I'm already very worried, Ty. I won't rest until I know you and Jack are both all right. Promise you'll call me?"

"Yes. All right." Distracted, he glanced around for his jacket.

She held it out so he could slip into it. Then she stood on tiptoe to look him straight in the eye.

"I love you, Ty. I'll be praying—for both of you."

"Yeah. Thanks." He glanced at Mac, a question on his face.

"Go. I'll handle things here."

Ty nodded. He turned at the door, studied Cassidy for a moment as if he wanted to say something, then shook his head and left.

"Oh, Mac. This is awful."

"It's worse than that, Cassidy." The old man flopped down into a chair, threw back his head and sighed.

"Worse? How?"

"Jack was on drugs."

"Drugs?" Understanding. Disbelief.

Ty was about to face a replay of his brother's rebellion.

"Oh, Lord." She squeezed her eyes closed and began praying.

Ty stared down at the lanky boy sprawled across his own bed, now softly snoring.

This time the flashback was from his own youth.

Donnie. It was happening all over again and there was nothing, nothing he could do to stop it.

No, that wasn't true.

There *was* something.

Ty had to get Jack out of here, away from the punks who'd sold him the junk, away from the same streets that had claimed his brother.

*And the Haven?* his conscience prodded.

"I'll find someone else to do Your work, God."

Ty checked every place in the boy's room where Jack might have hidden drugs and found nothing, which could mean it was the first time Jack had used. But once might be enough. He tiptoed out of the room, drew the door closed behind him and sagged against the frame.

"Oh, God, why?"

There was no answer. In truth he hadn't expected one.

His big easy chair sat in the corner. Ty sank into the soft leather, ignored the leather-bound Bible, too tired to read. Instead, he let his head sink onto his chest as despair took over.

Jack's actions tonight, the upcoming court case, the negative publicity that could be expected now that a reporter had seized on the story, the questions he'd had to field about his ability to help others when he couldn't help his own nephew—those were simply the last push toward a decision he actually welcomed.

It was time to leave.

Ty picked up the phone and dialed Elizabeth Wisdom.

# Chapter Thirteen

For a week Cassidy fought the heavy atmosphere, filling the Haven's kitchen with constant prayer.

But as the grand opening loomed, strain showed on everyone, especially Ty. Gone was the teasing man she'd first met. This Ty seldom smiled and never laughed. He pushed too hard and had lost weight he couldn't afford to lose. And he avoided her. Cassidy tried to talk to him many times, but he always had an excuse. In the mornings he disappeared, in the afternoons he counseled and in the evenings he and Jack left right after dinner.

Worst of all, Ty didn't go up on the roof anymore. Cassidy checked, found his telescope tightly wrapped under a thick tarp. The seating area looked abandoned, like no one bothered to use it. Doubts assailed her but she kept praying.

The morning before Good Friday, Cassidy slept in. By the time she arrived at the Haven, Ty was gone. He'd done that a lot lately, canceled appointments and disappeared. Cassidy was determined to speak to him as soon as he returned.

Jack's associations with others outside of school were limited. So when he and Red came sauntering down into the kitchen that afternoon, Cassidy couldn't believe he'd broken the court order right before the Haven's official opening.

"What are you doing here? School's not out yet."

"I've taken the afternoon off with my friend Red. It's our last afternoon together. You don't have a problem with that, do you?" His smirk told her he didn't much care if she did. "Don't worry—I'll be out of your hair soon."

"You know Ty will do everything he can to keep you out of jail."

"I won't be going to jail, Cassidy."

The cocky way he said it irritated her.

"You don't think what you did deserves punishment?"

"Yep." He grinned at Red, who didn't seem to share his forced joviality. "Lock me up and throw away the key."

She studied him. "Are you high?"

"No," he shouted, lurching to his feet. "Anyway, I'm not your business. Not yours. *Not his.*" His voice broke.

"Yes, you are." She touched his cheek. "We love you, Jack."

"Yeah, sure. My uncle Ty loves me a whole bunch."

"He does. Neither of us wants to see you make any more mistakes."

"Like moving to New York is going to help." His face contorted with rage.

"You're not going to New York." She stopped because Jack's face told her he was telling the truth. "He's sending you away?" Shock vied with hurt. Ty hadn't told her. "Oh, Jack, I'm sorry."

"Not me, us. He gets his big fancy practice and I get private school at some place where they straighten out rotten kids like me. We're leaving Sunday if the judge agrees to it today. That's what he's doing now."

Yesterday she'd asked Ty how the case was going, if the lawyer thought something could be worked out.

*"No news, Cassidy. Trust me, I'll let you know if any-thing changes."*

He'd lied.

Worse than that, he'd shut her out.

She'd trusted his promises of love, even thought that she might have a future with him. She'd made a mistake. Ty had betrayed her as surely as her father had all those years ago when he'd promised he'd come back home and he never had.

*Oh, God, how could You let it happen all over again?*

Fierce pain ripped through her heart and shot a bullet of agony to her brain. She grabbed the back of a chair, sank into it while her dreams imploded. He didn't love her. He couldn't. Love didn't lie.

"Cassidy?" Jack knelt in front of her, brown eyes teary. "I'm sorry I told you like that. I was mad."

She smoothed her hand over his glossy head, hugged him close.

"Oh, Jack."

"Don't cry, Cassidy. I didn't mean to take any drugs." He scrubbed the tears from his cheeks. "Somebody slipped it into the soda. At least I thought it was soda. Red said those guys were no good. She warned me, but I wouldn't listen."

Cassidy shot Red a watery smile of thankfulness.

"Why wouldn't you listen to Red, to me, to your uncle?"

"I wanted him to love me. I hurt so bad after my mom died, and I just wanted him to love me. But nothing is right. He's mad all the time. At me."

"He's your guardian. He's supposed to take care of you."

"He's my uncle. He's supposed to love me, too. But he can't."

"Jack, that isn't true."

"I heard him on the phone." His pain tore her heart. "I heard him telling his friend that I am such a mess that military school is the only thing that will straighten me out. He hates me because I cause him too many problems. He's trying to get better and I make him sicker. I don't mean to, but I do. Ty doesn't want me around."

He jerked away from her.

"When he asked me to live with him, I thought it would be fun—that we'd do things together, that he would be like my dad would have been if he hadn't died when I was a baby." Jack smashed a hand against his thigh. "Since I've been around, his nightmares have gotten worse. It's my fault he doesn't sleep."

"Ty loves you, Jack. So do I."

Jack shook his head, but didn't say anything more. He cast a quick glance at Red, then before her eyes, he seemed to alter, harden.

"I have to go." He walked toward her, hugged her. "I just came to say thank you. You've always been great, Cassidy."

"I'll see you tomorrow, won't I?" She drew his tall, lean body into her arms, trying to find comfort.

"Tomorrow? Yeah, uh, sure."

"I love you, Jack. If you ever need anything, you come find me. Promise?"

"Sure."

"I mean it."

"Okay. We're going upstairs." He wriggled away, headed toward the door. He paused there for a moment, then beckoned to Red and they left.

Minutes later, Cassidy heard the big door upstairs slam.

Cassidy wondered how long Ty had known he was leaving. He could have explained. Instead he'd deliberately kept his secret, refused to trust her. That wasn't love. Not the love she wanted or needed.

*When things got tough, Ty ran away. Just like her father.* How could she love him?

She hurried up to the roof to talk to the only One who understood her bleeding heart.

Surprised to find the door unlocked, Ty stepped onto the roof, struggling to adjust his eyes to the gloom.

"It's about time you showed up. It's going to storm."

She knew.

From the sound of her voice, Ty understood that Cassidy had learned of his plans.

The noise in the hallway—Jack must have overheard him on the phone.

"When were you planning on telling me? Or were you just going to leave and hope I figured it out on my own?"

"I wanted to get the details nailed down, to make sure it would actually happen before I told you." He touched her shoulder but she flinched away. "I didn't want to worry you."

He saw the tracks of her tears. But she wasn't crying now.

Cassidy was blazingly angry.

"Add that lie to the rest you've been telling. You didn't tell me because you knew I'd disagree, or because you didn't want to hear my opinion at all. You were doing what you always do, taking the easy way out."

"Now just a minute."

"Hear me out, Ty, because what you've done is a colossal mistake."

"It's a solution."

"To what? Your embarrassment over a news story? A way out of failing to make the Haven what you think Gail wanted it to be?" She hugged her arms around her waist, though the spring evening was warm. "All these months you've talked about God. Did you even bother to ask His opinion?"

He hadn't, Ty realized belatedly.

"I have to get Jack away from here, away from what he could become."

She shook her head, dark hair dancing in the breeze, silver eyes boring right through his veneer of composure.

"The problem is not Jack, Ty. It's not the Haven, either. The problem is you. You have no faith. Not in Jack. Certainly not in me and more importantly, not in God."

"I think I'll do better in New York."

Scorn tinted the edges of her laugh.

"You mean you'll hide there, until it gets too uncomfortable. Then you'll run away from New York, too."

Her words cut deep. "You don't have a very high opinion of me. I thought you said you loved me."

"That's why this hurts so much. I trusted you. I believed in you. I saw that when needed, you could set aside your problems, reach into your heart and draw out a wealth of compassion and generosity."

Her silver eyes lost their gleam, dulled by hurt. His fault.

"I saw you ache for wounded families and I thought, now there is a man who will never act as my father did. Ty will never lie to me."

Heat scorched his face.

"If this is about your restaurant, you could still have one in New York. A better one."

Cassidy shook her head. "No, I couldn't."

"There's nothing in Chicago that New York can't offer."

"I'm not going to open a restaurant. I don't believe that's where God wants me."

"Then—?" He didn't understand. She was giving up her dream?

"I do love you, but not even for you, Ty, will I walk away from God's will. I realize now that He wants me here, in the

Haven, making soup, frying doughnuts, whatever." She stopped, swallowed. "And I'm glad."

"You want to stay here?" It didn't make sense.

"As long as He wants. Having my own place couldn't match the joy I find here every day." For a few moments her face glowed, until she looked at him. "I thought we'd both be here. I guess I was wrong."

"I can't stay, Cassidy. The place chokes me, Jack is getting worse. It's not working out."

"Why do you think that is?"

He had no answer.

"When I first came here, Ty, you talked a lot about God. You kept telling me how much God wanted me to be whole, to be His child. Don't you believe He wants that for you?"

"It's different."

She smiled.

"It's exactly the same. But until you let go, quit manipulating and finally surrender everything to Him, I don't think you're going to find total healing. If I've learned one thing it's that He's God of all or He's not God at all."

"But I love you, Cassidy. I thought everything would be great—"

"Once you shipped Jack off to military school?"

"I don't know what to do with him," he exploded. "I don't want to lose another member of my family to these streets. I can't make him understand."

"Did you tell him you love him? Did you tell him that if you lose him to the same streets where Donnie died, that you would be devastated?" Cassidy stood so close he could breathe in her familiar fragrance, smell the hint of mint on her breath. "Did you tell your nephew that you will do anything in your power to save his life—because you can't imagine a future without him in it? Or are you too afraid to let Jack see how much you care?"

"I—I—" Frustrated, Ty shoved his hands in his pockets. "I'm doing the best I can."

"For you or for him?" A sad little smile tipped the corners of her lips upward then disappeared. "You live your life in fear, Ty. You scrape through. I feel sorry for you."

He hated that.

"I feel sorry because you taught me so much about learning to stop being afraid, to trust and let God take care of me, to depend on Him." She touched his cheek. "I wish you could do the same, Ty. Stop worrying about the bad things that could happen and focus on the good that God has in store. I hoped we'd be able to stay here, work together. I'm staying, but it won't be the same without you."

"I didn't mean to hurt you, Cassidy. I wanted to protect you."

"I know." She leaned forward, hugged him tightly for a moment then stepped back. "But that's the problem. People get hurt. You can't protect everyone."

"What are you saying?"

"I'm saying we trust that God is bigger than the bad things, bigger than the punks who slipped a drug into Jack's drink, or the drugs that took over your brother's world."

"Is that what happened?"

"Why not ask Jack?" She pointed up, toward the evening sky. "If God could create the glory of the heavens, if He could make the earth spin around the sun and the planets stay in their orbits, if He can direct the rain and the thunder, don't you think God can keep Jack safe? Don't you think He can help you, Ty?"

"You don't understand."

"I don't think *you* understand the God you serve." Her earnest voice grated on his raw nerves. "He can protect you and Jack if you let Him. And if something happens He'll use it benefit you. He can't do that if you won't trust Him."

"I know you can't forgive me. I've acted like your father and—"

"It does hurt to know you didn't trust me, Ty." Fat, glossy tears hung suspended on the ends of her thick black lashes, but Cassidy was smiling. "But don't worry about me. God gave me forgiveness for my father and He'll help me forgive you. I'll learn how to build my life again. It won't be as fulfilling without you, but I trust God. Do you?"

Her simple words burned away all his excuses. Even almost changed his mind.

Then lightning flashed across the sky. Thunder rumbled and sent him hurtling back into the past where fear crouched.

"We have to get inside."

He heard her voice, felt her drawing him along, pushing him through the door. She slammed it closed.

"I'm going home. Everything is ready for tomorrow." Cassidy fled, tears spotting her pristine white jacket.

She would make a new life.

Jack would find sanctuary in his school.

But Ty would be alone to face his ghosts. Even now the specter of panic spread its clammy fingers around his throat. His haven on the roof inaccessible, Ty headed for his office, desperate to stem the tide of fear.

He flopped into his chair, squeezed his eyes closed and regrouped. He was safe. He was fine. Nothing had happened.

An envelope lay on his desk. *To Uncle Ty.*

Ty read the note while fear exploded every last vestige of his control.

"Help me, God. What do I do now?"

Cassidy.

He barreled down the stairs, met her halfway.

"Jack's run away. He says he's sorry he embarrassed me and ruined things with you. He says I don't have to worry about him anymore, that he'll look after himself." Ty shoved the letter at her. "I have to find him. Before it's too late."

He heard the wobble in her voice. "Let's go."

At the doorway they ran into Red, talking to Mac.

"Listen to her," Mac ordered.

"We have to find Jack. I have an idea where, but they won't be there for long. They'll try to initiate him."

"Who will?"

"The Gators, a very bad gang."

Ty knew the name—Walter, Jack's friend, wore a jacket with that name. His blood ran cold. He reached for Cassidy's hand. "We'll take my car."

"Call my dad," Red told Mac. "Tell him where I'm going."

As he steered through the raging winds and torrential rain, Ty prayed as he fought off the PTSD. But when they had to wait at a red light, Cassidy's words on the roof returned and his stomach sank.

He could not remember ever telling Jack he loved him.

# Chapter Fourteen

"Please, God, help us."

Cassidy alternated between watching the road and watching Ty. A quiet sob from the backseat drew her focus.

"Why are you doing this, Red?"

"What you said that day at the planetarium—how I could be part of the problem or part of the solution." Red sniffed. "I introduced Jack to the Gators. I thought I was cool. If anything happens— The light's green. Why isn't he going?"

Ty's hands held the wheel in a white-knuckled grip. His eyes glazed, his lips moved, but Cassidy heard nothing.

"Ty? Ty!" She squeezed his arm. "Let's get Jack, Ty."

He blinked, then followed Red's directions. Moments later, they pulled up beside an old cement bridge. An orange glow shone through the downpour.

"There, at the far end, under the bridge." Red pointed.

Ty was so pale Cassidy thought he'd faint. She grasped his hand and held on as they moved through the people huddled under the sheltering bridge. Every time they came near one of the many burning barrels, Ty flinched and she knew his flashbacks were growing worse.

"God is here with us, Ty. Ask Him for help."

He didn't seem to hear her. She kept coaxing him onward, praying harder than she ever had.


So many bodies.

Ty knew in his brain that what he was seeing wasn't real, but he couldn't break free, couldn't shake the fear. Until he bumped into Cassidy.

"We're here to talk to Jack," Ty heard her say.

"You're not welcome here. Go home before there's an accident."

"Not until we speak to Jack."

Ty lifted his head. The rain splashed cold and hard against his face, snapping him back to the present. He glanced at the burly youth barricading their path and knew they were in trouble.

"Jack's my nephew. I need to see him."

"Jack doesn't want to talk to you. He's got us now. We'll look after him." The guy barked out a laugh then snarled, "Leave before we hurt you."

He had to do this. Ty tried again.

"Please, it's important. I—I want to tell him I love him."

A burst of laughter cut off his words.

"Leave, Do Gooder. Now."

So he'd failed. Again.

Ty gulped down defeat. He dared not push the issue. Not with Cassidy and Red here.

Then from behind a voice boomed.

"He's not going. Neither are the rest of us. Get the boy, Walter. Or do you need help?"

A gang appeared, knives flashing.

"Get out of here, Markovich. Before we make you."

"You and who else?" Irina's husband—Red's father—stepped in front of Ty. "I brought some friends."

Davis, Crank and three others moved forward.

"Get the boy. Now."

"You're finished, Markovich."

"No, you are, Walter. You and your friends aren't welcome in this neighborhood anymore. We don't want your drugs, your weapons or your violence. We're prepared to defend ourselves and our families against you. All of you."

Ty saw Jack huddled over the fire. *God, help me.*

"Jack?" He pushed his way past, intent on telling his nephew what he should have said months ago.

"You shouldn't have come. You'll get hurt. I didn't want that."

"I'm not afraid of them" he said, and he realized it was true. "I'm afraid you won't forgive me. I'm afraid you won't believe me when I tell you how much I love you, how much I want to make the world safe for you, so you won't have the same problems Donnie did. I'm sorry I didn't tell you before. I've been so scared something bad would happen that I forgot to trust God. Come back, Jack. We can start again."

"What about the judge?"

"We'll work it out. Together. I love you, Jack. You're my only family and I don't want to lose you. I want to be there when you graduate, when you get married and have kids."

Jack remained mute.

"I can learn how to be a parent if you can cut me some slack." Ty faltered but Cassidy's fingers met his, infusing him with determination. "I need you to help me work through this thing I've got. Could you give me a second chance, Jack?"

"You want *me* to help *you?*"

"Yes. I need you. I love you. Yes, I want you to help me."

Jack frowned, thought it over. Then he turned to the gang.

"My uncle needs me."

Cassidy squeezed his hand. Ty squeezed back, his heart full. Knowing Jack wouldn't want any show of affection here,

Ty followed Red and Jack to his car, still clinging to Cassidy's hand as he sent his thanks Heavenward. Behind them the men began explaining to the gang how things were going to change.

They dropped Red at her home first, then Cassidy. Ty watched as she hugged Jack, tears filling her eyes. She nudged his cheek with her knuckles, then climbed out.

"We need to talk," he said as he walked her to the door.

"You need to talk to Jack." A tremulous smile flashed. "I'll see you tomorrow for the opening. Good night." She unlocked the door.

"Cassidy?"

"Yes?" She faced him.

Ty leaned forward and kissed her hard and fast. "I love you."

Then he drove home for a long, heart-revealing talk with his nephew.

Ty didn't sleep that night, but it wasn't because of any dreams.

It was because of a tall woman with coal-black hair, silver eyes and a heart that hadn't given up on him.

All he could think of was Cassidy.

"Don't let me mess that up," he prayed.

## Chapter Fifteen

The grand opening of the Haven took place on Easter Saturday.

Cassidy's ears rang with compliments. Everyone said the hors d'oeuvres and the meal were a huge success. Irina, face beaming, insisted on staying the whole day. She checked the doors, switched off the lights, then hugged Cassidy.

"Thank you," she said, tears streaming down her face. Then she was gone.

Cassidy had hoped for a private moment with Ty, but he'd been going nonstop all day. No doubt he was still with Elizabeth, discussing his replacement. Her heart ached with loss, but Cassidy refused to be sad. This was God's work. He would bless it and He would give her the desires of her heart.

Someday.

"You still here?" Jack scanned the kitchen, handed her an envelope. "I was supposed to give you this earlier, but I got busy setting up those extra beds and forgot. I don't suppose there are any of those little tart things left?"

Cassidy hugged him and laughed. "Four, on the counter. Enjoy."

"I will." He hugged her back. "Thanks."

"You're welcome." She opened the envelope, slid out the sheet of paper.

*Dearest Cassidy,*
*What a huge success today has been, and an affirmation that God is at work.*

*You are an enormous blessing, as I knew you would be. I thank you for giving so much. I regret I've had to dash away. I'm opening a ranch in Texas for disabled children and there are so many details but I'll talk with you soon. P.S. I've lost my glasses. Could you check the roof, near Ty's telescope?*
*Much love,*
*E.*

Despite last night's kiss, Cassidy wanted no sappy farewells. But she couldn't ignore Elizabeth's request so she climbed the stairs to the roof. The door stood open, Ty's telescope in its place, uncovered, as if waiting for him.

Something moved in the shadows and she realized Ty was there.

"Hi."

"Hi, yourself." He rose, walked toward her. "You must be feeling very satisfied. That meal was spectacular."

"Thanks."

"Do you have a moment to talk?"

She nodded, steeled herself for another apology.

"I want to show you something." He led the way to the telescope, adjusted the setting. "Look."

Once her eyes adjusted to the lenses, Cassidy gasped as the red planet loomed large and spectacular.

"Mars at its best." He turned her to face him. "It reminds me of you."

"Mars does?"

"Uh-huh. You just keep on shining, whether anyone notices all you do or not." He brushed his hand over her hair, fingered the strands. "You are like Mars to me, a beacon I'm drawn to. For a while, I lost my focus, but you never did. You remained true and pulled me back to reality again."

"Ty, I—"

"I don't have all the answers I want or need just yet. I don't know how long the PTSD will last. Nor do I know what will happen with Jack."

Mesmerized by that crystal-blue gaze, Cassidy said nothing. When his hand cupped her cheek, she couldn't help leaning into it.

"I only know two things for sure. I trust God with the future and I love you, Cassidy Preston. Do you love me?"

"Yes," she whispered. She couldn't deny her heart.

His arms circled her waist as he drew her into his embrace.

"Would it be too much of a hardship for you if Jack and I stayed, if I helped you make the Haven a place where anyone who walks through the door will find God's love?"

"I—" She caught her breath when he placed his forefinger over her lips.

"You're the one who grounds me, Cassidy. I need you here to push me, to encourage me, to love me. Is that too much to ask?"

She grasped his wrist and drew his finger away.

"Are you suggesting a partnership, Mr. St. John?"

He nodded, grinned.

"You, me and God."

Cassidy touched his cheek, his lips, brushed her hand through his hair.

"It's a deal," she whispered, leaning forward. But Ty held back.

"There's just one thing."

"Oh."

"I come with a nephew."

"I wouldn't take you any other way." She tilted her head. "I believe a kiss is an acceptable way to seal this agreement. Or would you rather shake hands?"

Ty's kiss answered most effectively.

A meteorite shower lit up the Chicago night sky for several minutes, but the man and woman on the roof were too engrossed in their own little haven to notice.

\* \* \* \* \*

Dear Reader,

Hello, there! Welcome back to my PENNIES FROM HEAVEN series. I hope you've enjoyed visiting Chicago. I've been there several times and on each occasion I've been awed by this magnificent city and the variety of people and activities that make Chicago so exciting. I hope to return soon.

Cassidy and Ty's journeys took them into a deeper, richer, fuller relationship with God. Though neither of them knew what was in store for them when they came to the Haven, they ended up finding their hearts' desires. That often happens when we obey God and give Him our best. It may not be an easy road, but it is always one that's blessed. Check back next month for another of Elizabeth Wisdom's projects in *A Cowboy's Honor.*

I'd love to hear from you. You can reach me by e-mail at loisricher@yahoo.com, on the Web at www.loisricher.com or by snail mail at Box 639, Nipawin, Saskatchewan, Canada, S0E 1E0.

I wish you a spring filled with promise, a summer brimming with contentment and a lifetime of joy from the Father who loves us beyond measure.

Blessings,

*Lois Richer*

# QUESTIONS FOR DISCUSSION

1.  Cassidy made a promise to Elizabeth Wisdom to return to the Haven, but she wasn't truly committed at first. Discuss how doing our duty can often bring us joy beyond our expectations.

2.  Ty suffered post-traumatic stress disorder and repeatedly lived through an episode from his past. People are sometimes repelled by disorders because they don't understand them. Suggest ways we can become more accepting of those who suffer from this and other disorders.

3.  Cassidy refused to forgive her father for his treatment of her and her sisters. Was she justified? Are some things unforgivable? Is forgiving the same as forgetting?

4.  Because of his problems, Ty's tendency was to back off from doing that which bothered him most. Talk about the means we use to avoid doing things that push us beyond our comfort zones. How can we minimize our fears and live fully vested lives that open us to being used by God?

5.  Cassidy achieved top-notch status as a pastry chef in Europe. Yet she was asked by Elizabeth to work at a soup kitchen. Do you think that was beneath her, that Elizabeth should have found something else? Would it be embarrassing to you? Pose situations in which repaying a debt would cost you status and change the way people view you.

6. Cassidy's father wanted to reunite with her but she chose not to until she had the issue better settled in her mind. Was this wise? How would you deal with a father, friend or spouse who had wronged you years ago and returned to ask forgiveness?

7. Ty fought his lack of security by imposing rules that he thought would lead to predictable behavior. He was so busy protecting his nephew he forgot to tell Jack he loved him. Discuss ways parents can find a middle ground, when raising teens, that allows the teen freedom but also ensures strong family ties.

8. Red appeared many times throughout the book, often as a negative influence on Jack. Every parent faces the issue of peer pressure on their kids. Discuss your ideas on handling such potentially explosive situations.

9. In this story, the gang was violent, but kids often are misled by less obvious influences. How can we protect children from those who would lead them astray? Are churches effective at ministering to kids? How can you help?

10. Running away to escape from a bad situation is a normal human response but it seldom solves the root problem. Suggest positive and negative results that occur when people run away from their problems.

# HISTORICAL

## INSPIRATIONAL HISTORICAL ROMANCE

Amid the splendors of the Gilded Age, Neala Shaw suddenly found herself entirely alone. The penniless young heiress had no choice but to face her family's fatal legacy of secrets and lies. And as she fled from a ruthless killer, an honorable man unlike any she had ever known stood between her and certain death.

**Look for**

*Legacy of Secrets*

**by**

## SARA MITCHELL

Steeple Hill®

*Available April wherever books are sold.*

**www.SteepleHill.com**

LIH82785

# REQUEST YOUR FREE BOOKS!

## 2 FREE INSPIRATIONAL NOVELS
## PLUS 2
## FREE
## MYSTERY GIFTS

**YES!** Please send me 2 FREE Love Inspired® novels and my 2 FREE mystery gifts (gifts are worth about $10). After receiving them, if I don't wish to receive any more books, I can return the shipping statement marked "cancel". If I don't cancel, I will receive 4 brand-new novels every month and be billed just $4.24 per book in the U.S. or $4.74 per book in Canada, plus 25¢ shipping and handling per book and applicable taxes, if any*. That's a savings of over 20% off the cover price! I understand that accepting the 2 free books and gifts places me under no obligation to buy anything. I can always return a shipment and cancel at any time. Even if I never buy another book, the two free books and gifts are mine to keep forever.

113 IDN ERXA  313 IDN ERWX

| | | |
|---|---|---|
| Name | (PLEASE PRINT) | |
| Address | | Apt. # |
| City | State/Prov. | Zip/Postal Code |

Signature (if under 18, a parent or guardian must sign)

**Order online at www.LoveInspiredBooks.com**

**Or mail to Steeple Hill Reader Service:**

**IN U.S.A.:** P.O. Box 1867, Buffalo, NY 14240-1867
**IN CANADA:** P.O. Box 609, Fort Erie, Ontario L2A 5X3

Not valid to current subscribers of Love Inspired books.

**Want to try two free books from another series?**
**Call 1-800-873-8635 or visit www.morefreebooks.com**

* Terms and prices subject to change without notice. N.Y. residents add applicable sales tax. Canadian residents will be charged applicable provincial taxes and GST. This offer is limited to one order per household. All orders subject to approval. Credit or debit balances in a customer's account(s) may be offset by any other outstanding balance owed by or to the customer. Please allow 4 to 6 weeks for delivery. Offer available while quantities last.

**Your Privacy:** Steeple Hill Books is committed to protecting your privacy. Our Privacy Policy is available online at www.SteepleHill.com or upon request from the Reader Service. From time to time we make our lists of customers available to reputable third parties who may have a product or service of interest to you. If you would prefer we not share your name and address, please check here. ☐

LIREG08

# *Love Inspired*

# TITLES AVAILABLE NEXT MONTH

## Don't miss these four stories in April